WHEN THE TIME COMES AND OTHER STORIES

M.H. LEE

ISBN: 978-1-950902-98-9

ALSO BY M.H. LEE

When the Time Comes and Other Stories

The following short stories which are part of the collection are also available on an individual basis in ebook format:

The Bearer *

The Price We Pay *

Death Answered My Call *

Drowning In Their Darkness *

To Be A Hero

The Taste of Memory

In Search of a Frickin' Hero

By Your Side When the Sun Sets

---

*Titles with an * were also previously included in the essay and short story collection A World Dark & Cold which is no longer available for purchase.*

CONTENTS

INTRODUCTION

WHEN I PUBLISHED MY FIRST SHORT STORY COLLECTION IN 2013 I named it *A World Dark & Cold* because so many of the stories were about a thoughtless or cruel world that didn't seem to have much sympathy for the struggles of others.

Some of those stories I moved to this collection when I retired the old one. Stories like *The Price We Pay* about a man with a terminal illness who is forced to keep proving his value to society to get life-saving dialysis treatments. Or *The Bearer* which is about a girl who isn't even allowed to speak while she serves as a surrogate for a wealthy family.

Given how the world has evolved since then you'd think my stories would've become unbearably dark and ugly.

But surprisingly (for me) some have more of a note of hope than my prior stories did. Stories like *When The Time Comes* which is a very short piece about how we each have the power in the moment to choose our actions (or reactions). Or *In Search of a Frickin' Hero* which came out far more humorous than I'd planned.

It's not all sunshine and roses, of course. Depending on how you feel about creativity and trauma and memory, *The*

Taste of Memory may rankle. Or it may have you nodding along at the end. And *To Be a Hero* is a darker take on the commercialization of war than we're ever likely to actually see.

So, you know, be prepared.

Anyway. I hope you enjoy the collection. I didn't include essays about each story this time around. I figured I'd let them speak for themselves. But if you're curious about any of the stories, drop a line and I'll see what I can do in terms of providing an answer.

I will say that as of this moment *By Your Side When the Sun Sets*, which is about an aging dragonrider and his dragon who is developing something akin to Alzheimer's is probably the closest to my heart since I'm watching my own dog get older day by day. But I like every single one of these stories and I hope you will, too.

WHEN THE TIME COMES

You will stand in line, glancing at the person in front of you, noting their skin color, their eye color, their hair color, the way they dress, the way they stand, their age, their gender. (Or at least what you think it is.)

You will catalog that person, placing them into the boxes you know, the categories you inhabit.

You will ask yourself: Are they like me? Or are they *Other*? Foreign. Different.

Maybe they will look like someone you like. That high school crush, that kind nurse who always has a smile to spare.

Or maybe they will look like someone you hate. Your dreaded sister-in-law. That horrible boss who once made you work late even though your mother was in the hospital. Or that man on the bus who never gives up his seat for old people even though you know he sees them.

You will look at this person, this individual who is, at their deepest, most cellular level 99.9999% like you and you will decide.

You will name them friend. Or foe.

It will happen in an instant. You won't know you do this.

You'll be thinking about what you're going to make for dinner or the latest episode of your favorite television show.

You won't understand how this thing you do without even thinking will change the course of your life and the lives of everyone around you.

You will judge this person and place them in your little buckets of reality. And that judging, that choice, that way you see them will haze your interactions with them so that when that person turns to look at you, when their eyes meet yours, the haze of your judgement will color your perceptions of what they do.

They'll have done the same. Together, you will shape your future. Together, you will shape *our* future.

Remember this, when the time comes. We're depending on you to save us.

THE TASTE OF MEMORY

THE SMELLS ARE THE HARDEST TO REMOVE. THAT WHIFF OF cinnamon as she turns the corner in the early morning that takes her back to the first time he cornered her in the back of her mother's bakery when her mother was out on deliveries.

Or the zest of lemon that was on his hands as he covered her mouth and pushed her into the little office where her mother's bills and recipes were strewn across the table.

The core memory—that hour of violation—is easy to find and erase. Dmitri can cut and snip it away in a moment, stitching the before and after together as if that hour never existed. But what makes him a master of memory, what makes him the most accomplished memory eraser working, is the way he handles the smells. And the touches. The echoes that reverberate from that moment forward.

An amateur will stop with the core memory. Snip it out. Stitch it up. Collect their two-fifty and move on to the next. Snip, stitch, next, over and over again. Five minutes, ten, and they're done.

But a moment like hers. A moment of fear and desperation.

A moment when the world shatters into little tiny pieces that can never be pieced back together again…

That moment doesn't end there. It crashes off the walls of the future, like a hall of mirrors reflecting back, back, back to that one instant in time.

If she'd gone to an amateur to have her memory removed she'd never understand from that moment forward why the scent of cinnamon curdled in her belly or why the taste of lemon on her tongue made her want to curl under the covers and weep.

Dmitri continued forward from that moment, tracing her life, tagging every little shudder, every quick flash of recollection. Some were no more than an instant. Some lasted entire nights.

He trembled as he lived through those moments with her, at her side through the darkest moments of her life, taking them away so she'd never have to live them again.

She wasn't the easiest patient he'd ever handled. Those were the ones that involved grimy back alleys and rough hands and strangers that were never seen again, the places and people limited to that one awful day.

But she wasn't the most challenging either. Those were the ones where home and violation intertwined. Where a mother laughed, unknowing, while sitting next to the monster who came into a little girl's room at night. Where what should have been a safe space was anything but.

Some patients he had to turn away because even he, expert of memory that he was, could never extract every echo, every reverberation. Not without destroying them. Some still pleaded for him to do it. They didn't care. Wipe their mind clean. Take it all. Just, please, take it.

But he wouldn't. He couldn't. He did what he could. Smoothed out the sharpest edges. Took the worst moments.

But some patients he could never make whole again no matter how hard he tried.

This one, though. This one he could help. Even with the cinnamon and the lemon and the memories of her mother's bakery. This one was limited enough he could erase that man from her life. Give her back a future full of trust.

He wiped the sweat from his brow and took a sip of water before turning back to his task.

He'd long since given up on any other drink. The residue of others' memories colored every other taste. Coffee. Beer. Wine. Vodka. Tequila. They were all there. Even the sticky sweet taste of Kool-Aid.

The girl was lucky she'd found him when she had. Only two years since that moment but it had taken him six hours to find all the wisps and hints and tendrils of trauma that spread from that one point forward.

Cinnamon and lemon.

No one realized how often their lives were flavored by cinnamon and lemon. No one except the frail young girl resting in the chair across from him, her pale blonde hair plastered to her forehead as she twitched and squirmed, reliving the moments with him.

It was a brutal business, memory erasure. A true calling for those who did it the right way. To walk through another's pain, to own it as your own, and then to take it away from them but never forget it yourself…

At least it had just been the once. He could help when it was just once. And so recent.

The ones who waited decades; he couldn't help those people. The scents and touches died eventually. The edge worn off. But it was the thoughts he couldn't fix. All those quiet moments between this and that. All the times when they slowed enough to stop running. When they let the screams fill them up to bursting. All those moments of being overwhelmed by the past, of being drowned and swallowed.

After a certain number of years there were just too many.

He twisted his neck to the left and then the right and rolled his shoulders. Almost there. One more scent lingered softly in the background. One more thread of memory to gently disentangle. What was it?

He searched gently, probing at the original memory. It wasn't the flour. Or the slight scent of disinfectant. It wasn't aftershave or deodorant. It was…poppy seeds.

Of course. How had he not realized that was part of it, too?

He leaned forward and began the laborious process of tracing the scent of poppy seeds, tagging and eradicating each and every one.

Later, after she'd left, not even realizing how different she now was, how she practically floated on air as she walked out the door, he buried his head in his hands and wept. It was the best way he knew to clear away the residue of what he'd witnessed.

Pain shared is pain lessened. Or so they said. But what happens when you take on the pain of another and they no longer know it? When their pain becomes yours? Something private and dark that you hold close in a place no one else can see?

He stared at the framed picture on the corner of his desk— of a bright-eyed, blue-eyed child who smiled back at him from a beach somewhere that he'd long ago forgotten, her long brown hair tangled around her face. She must've been six or seven in the picture. He could almost hear her calling out to him.

"Daddy."

She'd been so happy that day. Before he'd failed to protect her from a darkness he didn't even know existed. Before the drugs. And what came with the drugs.

He'd just been a lawyer then. A single dad trying his best. He hadn't known who to trust. Or who not to trust. He hadn't seen the early signs. He didn't realize until she was so far down that path...

When he finally realized, he'd taken her to a memory expert. One of the best. Asked him to erase it all. Take it away. Bring back his shining girl.

But the man had been a hack. He'd scooped out her memories like her mind was a ripe honeydew. What she became after that was even worse.

She hadn't lasted six months.

That's when Dmitri found his calling. He quit his job, sold his hollow, empty house, and became a memory eraser. One of the best. He devoted himself to helping girls like his daughter. To giving back to them the life he couldn't give her.

Which is why his next appointment was so necessary. To help those too poor to pay for his services he had to take on work from those too wealthy for their own good.

Most were easy enough. "Can you please erase that memory of that one time I, horror of horrors, got a B on a test?"

Or "Can you please erase that memory of that boy who stood me up? It haunts me to this day."

The bad kiss. The scathing performance review. The awkward first date. Such travesties.

After the hours he spent witnessing real trauma, he almost hated them for thinking that their pain was anything worth mention.

But they paid well.

And when they paid well he could help the truly desperate.

He quickly washed his face and straightened his tie and

put on his suit jacket. (Appearances were so important with those types.) Closing his eyes, he took a moment to center himself and push away the residue of his past and then opened the door and nodded towards the pretty young blonde seated across from his receptionist. "Ms. Navery? Please, come in."

He appraised her as she seated herself across from him. Sometimes he was surprised by one of his higher-end clients. It wasn't always the poor who lived with darkness. Evil could happen just as easily behind the doors of a mansion as it could in a dirty alley somewhere.

But she didn't seem to be that type.

He braced himself for the request to please erase the memories of her pre-surgery nose because she could no longer live with the trauma of knowing she'd once been less than perfect as he asked, "How can I help you today?"

"I want you to give me memories."

He couldn't hide the twitch of his head. "Excuse me? You want to be *given* memories? Of what?"

It was technically possible to thread a memory into someone's mind. But it required even more skill to add a memory than to take one away. Because each moment after is defined by the moment that came before. You can't just drop a memory into the past and not expect there to be ripples. Not if it's a memory worth having.

She bit her perfectly plumped lip and held his gaze. "I want to be an actress."

"Okay. And?"

"And I need life experience. I keep trying out for these roles —you know the kind that young women are offered—but I have nothing to draw on. My acting coach tells me to think of a moment when I was really sad or really hurt or someone betrayed me. For example, if I'm acting out the part of a woman who just lost her boyfriend, I'm supposed to remember what it felt like when my dog died and use that sorrow. But I don't have any memories like that to draw on. I never lost a dog. Or a boyfriend."

He stared at her, frozen in place, not willing to move, the fire of righteous anger trying to burst through his skin and incinerate her.

"That seems like good advice," he finally managed to squeeze out between his clenched teeth. "You truly have no memories you can use? No disappointments? Ever?"

"No." She shook her head. "None."

He glanced at the list of patients that needed his services. He always kept a coded version right there on his desk for moments like this to remind himself why he didn't throw patients like this out the door. (Not that any had ever wanted him to add memories before, that was new.)

He had five patients on the list. Each would require at least a day of work. But right now he was barely keeping the lights on.

He needed the money.

He pressed his lips together. "I could perhaps give you a memory of a beloved dog that died." He'd had one himself when he was younger. A boxer who'd followed him everywhere until the day it tried to follow him to school and was struck by a car.

"Don't you have anything…worse?" she asked.

He gripped the chair arms. "Worse? Like what?"

She flinched and he had to force himself to unclench his hands. To rest them on his thighs and slow his breathing. A smile, though, was an impossibility.

"I'd heard that you work with the county. That you help remove memories from victims of crimes. I…" She bit that perfectly plumped lip and looked at him with those clear, unclouded green eyes. Eyes that had never seen a moment of horror like he witnessed every day. "I understand that you worked with that girl last month, the one in the papers. The one who was…"

"Get out." He stood, startling her and himself.

"But don't you see? I need those memories if I want to be an actress."

"Maybe you'd make a better model."

He wanted her gone. He wanted to grab her by the arm and drag her to the door and fling her down on the plush carpet in front of his receptionist's desk and tell her to never come back again.

"I can pay you. Whatever you want. Ten thousand? Twenty thousand?" She stepped closer. "A hundred thousand?"

A hundred thousand could save so many lives. And did she really deserve hers, this woman who sat there in the comfort of her perfect life and demanded something she couldn't understand? This woman who thought what his patients had been through was just material for her acting career.

It took all the strength he had, but he turned away from her. "No. I cannot do this. I will not do this. Leave. Now."

"I…Is there someone else you'd recommend?"

He turned on her, ready to strike. She clutched her purse to her chest as he gripped her arms so hard she cried out. He leaned close. "Listen to me. You have been blessed with a good life. Appreciate that. Don't destroy it. Let this go."

She pulled free of him. "I can't. I want this so much. Please, you're the best."

"No. Now please leave."

After she left he carefully lowered himself into his desk chair, shaking so hard he couldn't even pour himself a glass of water. A hundred thousand dollars. He could treat a hundred victims with that kind of money.

He should've taken it. Let her sacrifice herself so he could save all the others.

But no. Even if she didn't know what she was asking for, he did.

Dmitri continued his work, but he didn't forget her. Day in and day out as he scraped for the pennies to keep going, as he worked hours no sane human should work, as he struggled to relieve the darkness from soul after soul after soul, he thought about her.

About her offer.

About what a hundred thousand dollars could do. A hundred thousand dollars willingly offered.

It wasn't stealing. She'd get exactly what she wanted. And he'd be able to help so many.

But to do that to someone who didn't understand what they were asking for. How could he?

He consoled himself as he sat alone late at night in his dingy little apartment with the fact that it was all academic at this point. She'd asked, he'd refused, they'd never meet again.

But two months later she was back. Under a false name. He only knew it was her when he opened the door from his office and saw her sitting there, wide-eyed and shaking.

"Please. Don't make me go. I need your help." She rushed towards him, grabbed his arm, stared into his eyes with desperation.

"What do you want?" He shook her off.

"I can't…It's all jumbled up. I…I don't know who I am anymore. I don't know what's real."

He led her into the office and closed the door. Forced himself to sit behind his desk. Waited.

She slumped in the chair like a broken marionette.

"What did you do?" he finally asked, the words dropping into the silence.

She stared at him, wide-eyed as a deer. "I found someone to give me memories."

"Who?" His hand clenched.

He knew after all these years of this kind of work that there were those who'd do anything for money. Those who'd cut and trample on a mind for a buck. Or for their own pleasure. But whoever had dared to do this…

It was a sacrilege.

She shook her head. "I don't know. I remember visiting you and then that's it. I withdrew the money—I can see that in my bank account balance—but I don't know who I paid to do this. And now…" She clasped her arms tight to her chest. "It's like ants crawling on my skin. I know they're not my memories. But they're so real. Please. I need you to help."

"What do you want me to do?"

"Can you…blend them in somehow?"

"Haven't you learned?" he shouted.

She cowered before him. "Or you could just remove them? Please? I'll pay you the same? A hundred thousand?"

He nodded. Even though she'd brought this on herself, he had to help her. And the money…The money would let him keep his apartment. Let him keep his practice. "Tomorrow."

"Thank you."

Dmitri rolled his shoulders and sat back. Whoever had implanted the memories in her mind had shoved them into her brain like thumbtacks, each one a jagged point, so out of place it would be visible to even the most untrained memory specialist.

There were hundreds of them. Festering little spots of darkness scattered throughout her entire life.

Right there in the midst of her sixth birthday—her father had bought her a pony, she'd had that kind of childhood—the hack had inserted the memory of a brutal beating. It was the memory of someone much older, much bigger than a six-year-old, but it was there as real as the memory of Sparkles the pony.

It was like listening to merry-go-round music and then having someone insert the sound of fingernails on a chalkboard right in the midst of it.

Right after the memory of being declared homecoming queen whoever it was had shoved in a memory so vile Dmitri had to step away and shake and retch for a good five minutes.

He wondered as he stared at her, lying there, eyes closed, whether whoever it was had done it on purpose. As a punishment. He'd certainly had that moment of temptation. That moment of, "Do you really want to know what it's like? Here. See that? Feel that? *That's* what it's like."

Whoever it was had taken her money and done to her mind something more vile than all the memories combined. How she'd made it through a day let alone two months, he didn't know.

But he could fix it. And that's what mattered now.

The fake memories were actually easier to remove than real memories. There were no tendrils weaving themselves through every moment from that point forward. No scent associations. No touch memory. Just blots of poison dropped in the midst of what had been a really good life.

The kind of life he wished he could've given his daughter.

Where it became challenging, where he had to sweat and strain and work harder than he ever had before, was in the weeks after the memories were inserted. For two months, she'd fought against what she knew had happened but also knew hadn't happened. She couldn't reconcile it.

At some deep, root level she knew she'd had a good life. But the memories were real. The traumas real. That's when the drugs and the drinking started. If she was high enough she didn't have to think, didn't have to feel, didn't have to question the very nature of her reality.

For twelve hours he worked. Sweating, back hunched, only moving enough to take another sip of water.

But finally he had to do the worst. He erased her memories from that point forward. It was that or let her mind break. Two months wasn't so much. There was nothing too significant to lose. No death of a parent. No major acting role. She'd spent most of it curled up in bed or with a bottle. He left the vague outline of those two months but took away all the details.

When he was finally done he shook her shoulder gently. "Anna?"

She stared at him for a long moment. "Did you give me the memories? Can I be an actress now?"

"Anna. No. I..."

Why would she think that? But then he realized that he'd taken it all away. Of course. Why should she remember how those memories had almost destroyed her?

He should've left more. But it was too late now.

He gripped her shoulders and leaned forward. "Anna, I need you to listen to me. Please. You came to me for memories and I told you no. Do you remember that?"

She nodded. "But why am I here then?"

"Because someone else gave you the memories you wanted. But they hurt you when they did that. You came to me for help. You couldn't live with it."

"I don't remember."

"I know. I had to erase it. It was too much."

She tore free from his grip. "Why would you do that?"

"What?"

"Why would you take that away from me? That's what I needed."

"Anna…You don't understand what you did to yourself."

"You had no right. I wanted those memories. How dare you?" She stormed out of his office.

She was angry, but at least now she could be her old self. She could have a happy life.

And he finally had the money to help those who needed it. He hadn't even had to harm her to do it. He was content. At peace with his choices.

Until she came back to see him a month later.

"Anna. What do you want? Are you okay?"

She sat down across from him, her hands clenched tight in her lap. "I want the memories you took from me. I want the memories you should've given me the first time I asked for them."

"Anna. You don't understand. Those memories. You couldn't handle them. They were destroying you. That's why I had to take so much of those last two months."

Her hands shook, but she didn't look away from him. "I want those memories. I want to be an actress. If you won't give them to me then I'll find someone who will."

He leaned forward. "Last time you did that it almost killed you. Whoever did the work was a hack. You should've seen what they did to you."

"Then you do it. I'm going to do it anyway. You can either do it for me so I do it safely or you can refuse me and I'll find someone else."

He sat back in his chair. It was a devil's choice. The argument always made by the worst of the worst. Help me because I'm going to do it anyway. At least you can make it safe.

But it was also true. He was probably the only master of memory who could safely insert the types of memories she wanted.

"I'll pay you, of course," she sneered at him. "I'm not asking you to work pro bono. How's fifty thousand sound?"

"Last time you offered me a hundred." He wanted to swallow the words as soon as he uttered them, but they'd come out involuntarily.

"Yeah, well. Seems I'm down a couple hundred thousand in the last few months. For nothing. Fifty thousand. You give me the memories I want. Or I'll find someone who will."

He knew he should let her walk. He knew it. If she wanted to self-destruct, then he should let her. He didn't need to help her down that path. But he also knew he was probably her only chance at staying sane.

He bowed his head, praying for forgiveness from whoever gives it.

"Okay. Tomorrow."

The next day as they prepped for her session she was almost giddy, throwing out idea after idea at him. Could he give her an older professor who was a little too interested? What about an attack in a parking lot late at night? Something with a knife?

Idea after idea, she threw at him. Like it was a game. He felt that rage burn inside him again. All his patients who wished they could forget moments like that. All the ones who'd never sought his help and somehow managed to live with the darkness that overshadowed them.

And this woman. This woman talked about it like she was buying a new designer purse.

He understood for just a brief moment why the other doctor had done what they did. Why they'd poked each memory into her brain like a knife.

But he wasn't that kind of person. He couldn't inflict harm like that. So he chose the memory from the bakery. The one full of cinnamon and lemon. He layered it through her mind, tracing down every taste of cinnamon, every sight of a cluttered desk in a small room, every hint of lemon, and adding on that extra level of meaning. That extra depth.

He gave her a dead dog, too. A cute little yippy thing that didn't last long. He gave it parvo. Let it die after two weeks. But it broke her heart because she was only six and that puppy was her entire world while it lived.

He was disgusted with himself by the time he was done. He couldn't even look at her as she opened her eyes and beamed at him.

"The dog? Is the dog real? It feels real." She shook her head in awe. "Wow." She sat up and frowned. "Is that it? Is that all you did? Just one lousy dead dog?"

He opened the office door. "Margaret, could you please bring Ms. Navery a cup of tea? With lemon, please."

Anna glared at him, arms crossed. "I can't believe I paid you fifty thousand for one lousy memory of a dead dog."

"It should let you act the part of a broken-hearted girl-friend, shouldn't it?" he snarled.

"I wanted more!"

Margaret handed her the cup of tea and left. Glaring at him, Anna picked up the wedge of lemon and squeezed it into her tea. As the citrus scent filled the air she turned her head to the side, clutching at her belly. "What..."

She tilted her head to the side and stared at nothing for a long moment. "Was that you, too? Or is that...? Did that happen to me?"

"That was me. Now, please, leave and never come back."

"Do you have a bathroom? The lemon." She held her hands away from her body.

"There's one by the elevators. Please go."

He closed the door behind her and leaned his forehead against it. He'd done what he had to save her. If he hadn't done it she would've gone back to whoever hurt her the first time. But he could barely stand to live with himself, knowing what he'd done.

Taking the memories of that girl in the bakery. Giving that to Anna. Selling that trauma like it was a specialty vacation package. He felt dirty. Unclean.

He told himself he'd had to do it, but still...

A year later he saw her on the television. She'd changed her name to something more suiting a starlet—Cassidy Caine—and was being interviewed about her gritty performance as a teen prostitute in a new movie directed by a man known for "challenging" his actors.

So it had worked. She'd found the life experience she'd wanted so desperately.

He paused the interview to study her face. Had she stopped with the two memories he'd given her? Or had she found someone else to give her more? Or maybe she'd finally chosen the more traditional route of pills or booze or sex.

He knew better than most that it didn't take a hundred thousand dollars and a memory specialist to acquire the experiences she'd wanted. All it took was a few wrong turns. Around every corner and in every dark alley (or at least it seemed that way given his work) there was someone waiting to take advantage of the vulnerable. To push them further into the darkness they'd stumbled across.

He shook himself like a wet dog and turned off the television. What he'd done for her, to her, was in the past. He needed his focus. Today was going to be a challenging day. A young man who'd suffered the death of his parents, and then his grandmother, and then lived in a series of unfortunate foster homes, the last one so bad it had resulted in a court trial and six months of physical rehab.

It was a state referral. The treatment paid for out of the victim's compensation fund. Of course, the state being the state they'd only pay for removal of the last brutal beating. But Dmitri didn't care about that. He'd help the boy however he could. Take whatever memories the boy wanted to lose if they could be safely removed.

It was true, he couldn't afford the time it would take and he was once more scraping the bottom of the barrel and looking at a stack of past due notices, but this was who he was, what he did. He'd keep going until they hauled him out the door of his office and turned off the lights.

An hour later he sat across from the boy, James. The boy kept glancing towards the door to make sure it was still open. "Whatcha gonna do to me?" the boy asked.

"The court is paying for me to remove the memory of what that man did to you. I'm one of the best at what I do, so when it's gone it'll all be gone. It'll be like it never happened."

The boy kneaded his knees, never once making eye contact with Dmitri. "What if I don't want that?"

"You want to remember what was done to you?"

He stared at a spot on the floor. "No. But, maybe?" He finally glanced at Dmitri but then away just as fast. "It's..." He pressed his lips tight together and furrowed his brow. "I don't want it to happen again."

"It won't. That man is in prison. He'll never hurt you again."

The boy shook his head, denying Dmitri's words. "But if you...if you take away the memory, how will I know? Next time?"

Dmitri's heart broke a little bit at the question. Not a new one, unfortunately.

He leaned forward. "James. I know it's hard to believe this right now, but there won't be a next time. That man who hurt you was not like most people."

James stood and paced the room, his hands clenching and unclenching. "Yes he was. You think he was the first one who hurt me?" He shook his head. "You take it away, I won't be able to know. I won't...I'll let it happen again."

"You didn't let this happen."

James slashed his hand through the air. "I don't want you to take it away. I don't want you to take any of it away."

Dmitri rested his hands on the top of his desk. "James. You can't live with this festering inside of you. It'll destroy you."

He turned on Dmitri. "Not if I don't let it. What do you

think people do who can't have their memories erased? They learn to live with it. They get over it. I'll do that."

The fire in the boy's eyes was so intense, Dmitri bowed his head. "Very well. But if you change your mind…"

"I won't."

After James left, Dmitri sat back, wondering if he'd ever see the boy again. It was true that not everyone was broken, not even by the worst experiences. But he worried for the boy.

Because many were. And many suppressed it for so long there was nothing to be done by the time they sought help.

It was patients like James that made Dmitri worry that maybe he was doing something wrong. He saw all the good he did. The pain he took away. The suffering. The echoes.

But what was lost? Was he sending his patients back out into the world to be hurt again? Was he stripping away something that would drive them to greatness? Something that would make them stand above the rest and accomplish something amazing?

He searched for Cassidy Caine online. The reviews on the movie were good. Not just good, excellent. Award-worthy.

Two little memories and she'd done that with them.

Had she been right? Was it the memories that had given her the edge? Or had that been inside her all along?

He didn't know. All he knew was he took away the pain and that was a good thing.

Six months later she came to see him again. Her face was on the cover of every major magazine. She was the "it" girl of the week.

Her eyes skittered around the room. Her hands twitched. Drugs? Alcohol? Or memories?

"How can I help you, Anna?" he asked, tensing for what he knew was coming.

She sprawled in the chair across from him. "I need more."

"No."

"You have to give them to me. I need them. I have a big audition coming up. The dog and the bakery aren't enough anymore."

"No."

"You'd let me go somewhere else? I can, you know. I have enough money now to pay anyone anything. But you saw what they did to me last time. Do you want that on your conscience?"

Of course she'd make the same argument. Why not when it had worked so well the last time?

"I'll pay you two hundred and fifty thousand."

If he did this, she'd never stop, never quit wanting more memories. She'd always want to go darker, go deeper. And he'd give it to her because if he didn't she'd go to someone else, someone who'd hurt her.

He'd seen the movie. She was good. She was really good. A talent. A star. But if he let her walk out of his office someone else would destroy that. The way someone had destroyed his daughter.

He had to help her.

"Tomorrow," he said.

Dmitri stared at Anna's face as she rested before him. She looked so young, so innocent. And yet, like so many before her, she didn't want that. She was in a headlong rush towards a dark future and all she wanted was to go faster.

He closed his eyes and begged for forgiveness for what he was about to do.

For the next eight hours he worked on her mind. Not implanting new memories like she'd wanted. No, that he would not do again no matter how good the result. Instead he sorted and sifted her memories, looking for every little moment of inspiration that had led her to his door.

That first movie she'd seen when she was eight that made her want to be up on the big screen, too. The middle school play where she was the lead and they gave her a standing ovation. That first pure note she'd sung in music class.

He found each one and dulled the edges. Rubbed away the thrill and passion that had driven her forward.

It was no different, really, than what he did for his normal patients. Finding that moment that changed it all and erasing all the paths that spun out from there. In her case he dulled them instead of erased them. Layered on boredom and disinterest, stole joy and that soaring soul-feeling when something is perfect.

He also took back the bakery memory, but he left the dog. Let her have something to work with.

It made him ill to do what he did, but he was saving her from herself. Someone had to take away that horrible need that propelled her to want his services. It was something so bright and potentially pure, but she'd turned it inward until it was something dark and evil that would eventually destroy her.

It had to go. Or so he told himself.

Six months later her career was over. She'd left the business, her surprise turn splashed across all the magazines and every celebrity gossip site. The talking heads who talk about people for a living expressed their surprise. She'd been so good, so driven.

But now she wasn't.

They lamented the loss of such a wonderful talent, but Dmitri celebrated the survival of the girl with a good life.

He closed down his computer and welcomed his next client.

"Tell me, how can I help you today?" he asked the nervous young man sitting before him, hands clasped in his lap.

"I was wondering, can you insert some memories for me? I'm writing a novel, but I just can't get the level of emotional depth I want. I can pay...."

DROWNING IN THEIR DARKNESS

Freya's life was simple—helping her parents on the farm, spending a few quiet afternoons down by the river with her sister, Jadzia, and occasionally riding into town with her father.

She knew one day she'd marry Devlin—the boy from two farms down the road—and they'd spend their days raising a family just like her parents had before her, and theirs before them.

All of that changed the summer she turned fifteen.

Freya started to feel "it" that summer.

She couldn't explain exactly what "it" was, just that she no longer felt in control of herself when she was around people. When they focused their attention on her she felt herself bend or flow into someone else—someone more like what they wanted her to be.

The first time Freya really noticed the change was on a day so hot that all she wanted was to lie in her room until the afternoon rains blew through.

For whatever reason, Freya's mother had decided to make a blueberry pie that morning. As Freya lay in bed, fanning herself with the brim of her bonnet, she wrinkled her nose at the stench.

She'd always hated blueberries. They were squishy and gross and she'd never understood why people thought they tasted good.

"Freya! Come down here."

As lethargic as she'd been a moment before, at the command Freya jumped out of bed and raced downstairs to join her mother and sister in the kitchen where her mother thrust a plate full of steaming blueberries and flaky crust in front of her. "Try some pie. I'm sure you'll love it. I used cinnamon."

Instead of turning her nose up in disgust like she would have normally, Freya ate the pie, savoring every bite.

Freya eating something she didn't like wasn't entirely strange. She'd always been willing to do little things to make her family happy—give her yellow hair ribbon to her sister, listen to her father tell the tale of the Old Man and the Cooper for the tenth time, help her mother organize the cellar.

What was different—and what she only realized later when she finally stopped to think about it—was that on that particular day, when her mother had asked her to eat the pie, she hadn't forced herself to eat it to please her mother.

No. During those few moments, Freya had *wanted* to eat the pie.

And she'd loved it just like her mother had said she would.

As her mother had watched with eager anticipation, Freya had shoveled bite after bite of blueberry pie into her face and told her mother how delicious it was.

And she'd meant every word.

Late that night, lying on her bed as a cool breeze finally cooled her skin and Jadzia snored in the corner, Freya thought about what had happened in the kitchen and wondered if maybe she'd changed.

These things happened sometimes. She was growing up after all.

Maybe she liked blueberries now.

To test her theory, Freya snuck downstairs and found the remainder of the pie.

She pulled the plate close, inhaling the sweet scent of pastry and berries, and...gagged. It was all she could do not to retch at the foul smell of the most awful fruit in the world.

She almost dropped the plate on the floor in her hurry to get away from it.

No. She hadn't changed. She definitely still hated blueberries.

Except, it seemed, when her mother told her she'd love them.

Freya worried about this change in herself, but she didn't tell anyone about it. It was just blueberries after all.

But it wasn't just blueberries.

One sweltering mid-summer morning, when she and Jadzia took a picnic lunch down to the river, Freya finally began to see how powerful "it" was.

As they sat there in the sweltering heat of the day, Jadzia eyed the cool water flowing nearby. "We should go for a swim when we're done."

Jadzia had always loved to swim. She was like a steelhead fish, slithering through the water with perfect ease.

Freya shuddered. "You can, but I'm not going."

She had never taken to the water. She hated it. She wouldn't even stand within reach of the bank, it scared her so much.

So, when they'd finished eating and Jadzia started to strip off her clothes to go for a swim, Freya knew that she wouldn't join her sister no matter how hot the day or how refreshing the water.

Except…

Not a moment later, when Jadzia turned to her and said, "Come on, Freya, let's go for a swim," Freya went.

She didn't even hesitate.

The little voice in her head that had warned her of the danger was gone. She *wanted* to swim with her sister.

Until, that is, Jadzia ducked under the water and Freya found herself alone with the strong current swirling around her hips. She panicked as the water tugged and pulled at her feet, trying to flee back to shore before it could take her. But she slipped, the icy cold water dragging her under, filling her throat as she tried to scream and it pulled her away from the shore.

As the river threw her into rock after rock, Freya wondered what had made her do something so foolish? She knew better, so why had she gone into the river?

She would have drowned that day if the hunter hadn't rescued her. He saw her bedraggled body in the water and barreled in to grab her with arms the size of tree trunks, withstanding the deadly flow of the water as if it were nothing.

Freya was so grateful to him—he had saved her life after all.

But…

As he wrapped her half-naked body in a blanket, Freya felt pulled by his will. He *wanted* her to be grateful. And he wanted…

He wanted her to show her gratitude to him by…

By doing something she'd never done before. Something she'd always been told she should never do until she was married.

But, in that moment—just Freya and the hunter there alone in the woods—she didn't hesitate. It was what he wanted. So she gave it.

There were no doubts, no worries. Not in the moment

It was only later, when he left her alone by the fire to check his traps, that Freya regained herself.

And then…

Then she finally knew that something was terribly, terribly wrong.

She remembered what she had done with the hunter and how she had felt when she did those things. In the moment, with him looming above her, his hands grasping her hips and his breath heavy on her face, she had wanted it.

Enjoyed it even.

It had been her choice. He hadn't forced her.

But…At the same time…

It *hadn't* been her choice. Not really.

Without the hunter's need to drive her, she would have never done any of it.

Even now. Even with the memory of the pleasure she'd felt in the moment, it wasn't what she wanted.

Freya just wanted to go home.

She resolved to ask the hunter for help when he returned.

But she didn't. Because he wanted her to stay.

So she did, never once telling him how she missed her family or how the things they did in the dark of the night weren't things she wanted.

Because while he was there, she didn't miss them. She only wanted what he wanted, which was for her to stay and love him.

So she did.

Until one day the hunter once again left Freya alone and it all came crashing down on her.

How had she forgotten her friends and family so easily? They must think her dead, lost to them forever. She knew she needed to go home. And she knew she wouldn't tell the hunter if he came back, because he didn't want her to go.

So she fled.

She ran and ran and ran through the forest, branches lashing her face, stones cutting her feet, sobbing, half-blinded by her tears.

She didn't even know where she was going—just that she needed to get away.

The hunter wasn't a cruel man, it wasn't his fault. But what she'd become in his presence, it wasn't who she wanted to be.

Freya finally stumbled out of the forest as the sun cast one last angry swath of red across the sky, silhouetting a farmhouse in the distance.

She started towards the dwelling, longing for a hot meal and company, but stopped herself there on the edge of the wood, the lure of comfort calling her forward.

What if...

What if it wasn't just the hunter? What if what had happened with him could happen with anyone?

And what if the person in that house wanted something from her, too?

She wouldn't find her way home. She'd be trapped—captive to their will.

She might never get home if that happened.

She couldn't risk it.

Freya snuck into the hayloft of a nearby barn, wrapped herself in a scratchy horse blanket, and cried herself to sleep.

What was she going to do?

When Freya finally limped her way home the next day—her feet shredded to ribbons, her skin slashed where tree branches had cut her flesh—there was a large group of men in front of her home.

Freya flinched as she saw them from the top of the hill.

She couldn't go down there. Couldn't let their wants and needs pull at her the way the hunter's had.

But it was too late.

"Freya!" Her father ran towards her.

She met him halfway, the power of his need to hold his little girl driving her steps.

"Oh, Freya, we thought you'd drowned." He squeezed her so tight she could barely breathe. "We thought you were dead for sure. We looked and looked for you. What happened?"

Freya stared into her father's worried eyes and she told him what he wanted to hear. "The water swept me away. I finally washed ashore and I've been trying to make my way back here ever since."

"Alone?" her mother asked, having finally joined them.

"Yes."

"Where did you sleep last night?" Her mother watched her, eyes narrowed in suspicion.

"In a barn."

"Why didn't you ask for help?"

Freya felt the tug of her mother's desire to hear the truth, but her father's need for his daughter to be safe and untouched was stronger. Freya snuggled into his embrace, anchoring herself to that desire for things to be simple and clean.

"I just wanted to get home," she replied. "If I'd stopped at the farm, they might have kept me there."

"Enough questions, Lorelei. Come along, Freya. Let's get your wounds tended to." Freya's father led her through the crowd. The men's desires pulled and tugged at Freya like a river, threatening to drown her, but her father's presence was like a fortress, protecting her.

***

That afternoon, Freya found herself alone in the bedroom she shared with her sister. Her limbs were wrapped in strips of linen soaked in healall and she'd been told not to walk unless absolutely necessary for at least a week.

Freya lay on her bed, staring at the ceiling as she cried silently, the tears rolling down her cheeks and pooling in her ears. What was wrong with her?

The things she'd done—going in the river, being with the hunter—that wasn't her.

And yet it was.

Because she hadn't hesitated. She hadn't doubted for a moment.

They'd asked and she'd acted.

She hated Jadzia for asking her to go for a swim. Jadzia knew how scared Freya was of the water. It was all Jadzia's fault.

She resolved to confront her.

But when Jadzia came in a few hours later and collapsed on her knees at the side of Freya's bed, taking Freya's hand and begging for forgiveness, Freya forgave her immediately.

It was what Jadzia wanted after all.

The next day, Freya was watching the slow progression of the sun across the wall when her mother came to see her.

Her mother's need to know the truth was so palpable that Freya almost blurted out the words the moment her mother entered the room. But just as Freya opened her mouth to tell her mother everything her mother's reluctance to hear those words slammed into her like a wall.

Her mother lowered herself to Jadzia's bed and watched Freya for a long time. She started to speak a few times, but never managed more than a word or two before lapsing back into silence.

All Freya could do was wait, captive to her mother's conflicting desires.

Finally, her mother left, never having said more than one or two words in all the time she'd sat there. Freya thought about calling her back and demanding to know what was happening, but she didn't.

She longed for her mother's comfort, but what she'd felt from her mother had been as much fear and revulsion as love.

Freya tried to escape into sleep, but that only brought nightmares. Terrible vision after terrible vision where she was powerless to exert her will.

She jumped off a cliff with her arms spread wide in joy while her sister watched and laughed. Lay with nameless man after nameless man, lost in their need for her, unable to assert herself, to say no, the part of her that watched knowing it wasn't what she wanted, but the part of her that acted doing so freely.

She awoke to the darkness of twilight and threw up, her body crumpled in on itself in pain and horror.

She didn't know what was happening to her. What she did know is that she didn't want to be what she was becoming.

She stood. She had to act now. While she was alone and untethered by anyone else's needs.

Freya crept her way down the back steps and into the kitchen. Her feet burned with fire at every step, but she ignored the pain. It was temporary—a necessary sacrifice to buy her freedom.

She could hear the voices of her family in the front room—

her father's deep rumble accompanied by the high-pitched laughter of her sister and the murmur of her mother cautioning them to be quiet.

Freya turned away from them and walked towards her mother's small workroom. Somewhere amidst the dried herbs and potions she'd find the solution she sought.

Her mother wasn't a trained healer, but people often came to the house to have her tend their ills. She had a certain affinity for others that put them at ease even before she administered her cures. And she was always right about what ailed them even when the person was too embarrassed to tell her the truth.

Freya tried to be quiet as she rustled through the various tinctures and tonics that lined the narrow shelves, looking for the black berries of the nightshade plant. She'd picked them just the week before, so there should still be some left.

Freya found them at last in a mottled glass jar on the top shelf. Her fingertips had just touched the jar when she found herself frozen, unable to move.

"Freya! What are you doing?" her mother's usually sweet voice was harsh.

"I came in here for the nightshade berries. I was going to eat them so I could die."

As she turned to face her mother, Freya saw the trail of bloody footprints she'd left on the floor.

Her mother's face was carefully neutral, but Freya felt the whirlwind of emotion hidden behind those calm blue eyes. "We need to talk. Wait here."

As her mother left, Freya turned back toward the jar of deadly black berries.

"Blast it!" her mother said, returning. "Come with me."

Freya obediently followed her mother out to the front room.

"Freya, dear, feeling better?" her father asked.

"Yes, much," she replied.

And she was, despite her bleeding feet and the bottle of poison she'd been forced to abandon just moments before. Because he wanted her to be better.

Freya's mother stepped between them. "Clive, I want you and Jadzia to run to the Bunderson's farm and pick up some eggs."

"Can we do it tomorrow?" he asked, clearly puzzled by this unusual request from his wife.

"No. I need you to do it now."

"Why? What's wrong?"

Freya tried to respond, but her mother's desire that she stay silent prevented her. She whimpered, torn between their competing needs.

"Go, Clive. Now." Her mother's voice was like a horsewhip.

He left immediately.

Freya's mother washed and bandaged her feet once more, never uttering a word. It was all Freya could do not to cry out at the roiling emotions that battered her. Love, fear, hatred, disgust…

Finally, when the bloody signs of Freya's passage had been erased and all seemed as good as new, Freya's mother sat down across from her.

"I was afraid this would happen." She stared at the rag she was twisting between her fists. "My sister was like you.

"It took us time to realize what was happening. She was often alone, running father's herb shop, so we didn't know at first. But it was a small town, so it didn't take long for the rumors to reach our ears. Rumors about how if a man went to the herbalist when Tanya was alone he could get far more than just a tincture to cure his headaches. About how she would be anything he wanted her to be—always willing, always ready."

Freya's mother glanced at her and then away again. "The beautiful girl with long brown hair and green eyes who could and would please any man…"

Freya's mother spat to the side and Freya flinched. Her mother had never spit in front of her before.

"I didn't want to do it, Mother. I mean, I did. He didn't…he didn't force me. I did it willingly. But, I wasn't myself."

"I know."

"You do?" Freya looked for some sign of compassion or understanding, but found none.

"You're an Empath, Freya. Like I am. But you can't control it. Where I can sense a person's general mood and expand my awareness to feel what they feel, you…You are subsumed by their will."

Her mother stared out the window. It was almost dark now. Freya's father and sister would be home soon. "I suspected it the day I gave you that blueberry pie. You ate it so enthusiastically. I started to wonder. I started to watch you."

"I can resist it sometimes," Freya said, silently begging her mother to look at her. "People don't always want something from me. And sometimes they want more than one thing from me. Like you on the day I returned. You wanted to know what happened in the woods, but you didn't. And Papa wanted me to be safe and unharmed, so I was able to tell the lie." She wanted to reach out and grab her mother's hands, but couldn't.

"It was much the same way with my sister." Freya's mother still wouldn't look at her.

"Then I'll be okay? I can fight this?"

"No."

Freya felt an urge to end it all, sparing her mother having

to deal with this, and an equal urge to weave flowers into a crown and sing "Ring Around the Rosie" like she had when she was little. Before…this.

"Mother…" Freya managed to say around the pain from her mother's conflicting desires.

"Sorry, Freya. Be calm. Relax."

"Can we fight this, Mama?"

"We can try."

"But you don't believe we'll be able to?"

Freya's mother finally looked at her. Her expression was so sad, so defeated, that Freya wished she'd continued to study the rag in her hands.

"It's the men, Freya. You're right. Most people don't want much from anyone else. Or what they want is so disjointed that you can find your own path through their needs. But the men… Especially once they know what you are…what you can give them…"

"Then we don't let them know." Freya reached out and took her mother's hands.

"Of course. You're right. We just won't let anyone know."

Her mother squeezed her hands, but Freya knew she didn't believe it.

It actually worked. For a while.

Freya stayed on the farm and made sure to avoid anyone except her family.

Freya's sister and father didn't understand what was wrong with her, but they humored Freya's mother. And when Freya started to act odd they left her alone and let her find herself once more.

Sometimes, Jadzia got bored and used Freya's weakness

against her—mostly by getting her to do the messy chores like mucking out the horse stalls. Jadzia saw no harm in it since in the moment Freya was always more than happy to comply and she could never tell her sister later how upset she was.

Freya tried to resist, but she never succeeded.

She couldn't even tell it was happening until it was over and by then it was always too late.

It wasn't annoying, but it wasn't all that bad. Not until that early fall day when they left Freya alone on the farm. Just for a few hours. Not like they could watch her forever.

Not like anyone was going to come by.

Except, someone did. Hakan, the butcher's son, stopped at the farm on his way to market. He was a nice boy—a little big and awkward, a little too friendly, but not a threat.

"Not a mean bone in his body" as the grandmothers said.

Freya tried to hide from him, but he'd already seen her and tracked her into the barn.

"Freya! I haven't seen you in ages. How have you been?" He smiled as he approached her.

"Hakan! I've been good, thank you."

As he came closer, she realized she really liked him. Really, really liked him. Liked his kind eyes and broad shoulders. His slow way of speaking.

He stepped closer. "I've been so worried about you. No one's seen you since the river accident."

"I know. Mama and Papa didn't want me to wander too far. They're worried something might happen to me." She smiled up at him, stepping closer as well.

He reached out to touch her face and she didn't step away

from him. Instead, she leaned up on tippy toes to kiss his lips as he stared at her in awe and disbelief.

His arms circled her waist, pulling her deeper into the kiss.

And then he was bearing her down to the straw and her world became one of satisfying his need. Later, she could remember little bits of what happened. His mouth on her body. Hers on his. The dust that danced in the afternoon sun. The smell of horses and sweat as they came together in the heat of the afternoon.

Hakan left her with a gentle kiss and a big smile.

Freya ran to her room and buried herself under the covers, shaking. Her mother had been right. She'd lost herself in the needs of the first man who wanted her.

It hadn't been *bad*.

Hakan was nice, and he genuinely liked her. He'd been so grateful, so gentle.

And she'd wanted him, too, in that moment. Her body had been freely given.

But…

She had never wanted Hakan before. Not like that.

And she still didn't.

She sobbed into her pillow, hoping she'd never see him again.

He came back, of course.

He didn't know. He thought she loved him. He thought she wanted him.

And she did—when he was there.

And then one day Devlin came to see her.

Devlin, the only boy she'd ever wanted.

He was so angry, so upset.

"Tell me it isn't true, Freya. Tell me you haven't been with Hakan."

Freya collapsed at his feet, hugged his legs, and swore that nothing had happened. Devlin was the only one for her. Always had been. Always would be.

Devlin pulled her to her feet and clung to her. "I'm sorry I ever doubted you, Freya," he said as she wept on his shoulder.

"It's okay, Devlin. I love you. Only you. I always have."

And she did love him. Always had. Always would.

She'd wanted to tell Devlin the truth, but she *couldn't* because he didn't want to hear it.

He loved Freya as he thought she was—pure, untouched. And his need for her to fit that image was so strong that she couldn't break free of it.

She lived in dread of the day Hakan would return and she'd betray Devlin again.

But Hakan never came back.

Britt, his closest friend, came instead. And Britt's brother, Soren.

They found her alone in the barn.

Britt cornered her near the tack room. "You lied, Freya. Why would you tell Devlin that you'd never been with Hakan?

Hakan loved you. Do you know what Devlin did to him? Beat him within an inch of his life. That's what. Because of you. Why, Freya? Why would you do it?"

Freya told him. All of it. About the blueberry pie and the river and the hunter. About Hakan and Devlin and even about why she was answering his question.

Britt listened in disbelief, his mouth hanging open.

Soren listened, too, but he listened with a cruel smile on his lips, his eyes roving her body as she spoke. When she was done, he stepped closer. "So, you enjoyed it? You enjoyed being with Hakan? And with the hunter?"

"Yes. At the time…"

"You'd enjoy being with anyone then." He took a step closer, reaching for her.

"Yes." Freya stepped into his grasp, her hands reaching for his clothes.

He shoved her back against the wall. "What if I didn't want you to enjoy it? What if I wanted you to scream and fight back?"

She glared at him. "Then I'd fight you."

"Good." Soren's smile bloomed. "Britt, guard the door. Freya and I are going to have a little fun."

Soren grabbed Freya's arms and shoved her into the tack room. She fought and screamed, but not so loud that anyone would actually hear her and not so hard that she'd manage to free herself. Soren didn't want that.

No, he wanted something else entirely.

And Freya gave it to him. She couldn't do anything else.

Soren left Freya crumpled in a heap—a handful of dull copper pennies strewn in the hay at her feet.

"Thanks, whore. I'll be back."

Freya lay there, her clothes shredded, feeling the aches throughout her body, remembering.

Remembering how Soren had grasped her flesh and whispered obscene things in her ear. How she'd *wanted* him to do those things.

She'd even begged him for more.

But that wasn't her. It wasn't.

Was it?

Soren came back.

And he brought friends.

Freya dreamt of the men every night. She couldn't get away from them even when she was alone.

She remembered the pleasure she'd found with them. Or at least with the ones who wanted her to feel pleasure. With the others…

She shuddered as she flinched away from the memories, wondering if this was who she was, someone who changed to please those around her.

Sweet and innocent for her father, steady and quiet for her mother, generous and helpful for her sister.

And for the men…

Whatever they wanted her to be.

Sweet and shy.

Bold and brazen.

Victim.

Whore.

Maybe she really was all those things?

But she knew.

Somewhere deep inside, she knew.

———

She lived for the days when Devlin came to see her. For the days when she could be his pure, sweet Freya. Untarnished. Untouched. Just a young girl who would one day marry the boy she'd always loved.

———

Some of the men Soren brought to her were older men—men with wives and babies at home that took their pleasure and threw coins at her without looking back, ashamed of themselves and disgusted with her, hating a woman who could so freely give herself to fill their needs.

She hated herself, too, while they were there.

And after. After, she scrubbed her skin raw, trying to get rid of the feel of their greasy bodies against her skin.

———

And then, one late fall day as the leaves died and pooled on the ground, came the moment when she could no longer be everything to everyone.

It was no longer warm, but not yet winter, and Freya was cleaning the kitchen when Soren found her.

He was alone. He liked to have her to himself every once in a while. Liked to do things to her that no one else should see.

He shoved Freya against the table, not even bothering to take off her dress, and tangled his hand in her hair, pulling back until her neck was bent at a ninety degree angle, willing her to scream.

She did.

That's when Devlin found them.

"Freya! What's going on here? Soren! You get the hell away from her."

"She wants it, Devlin. Don't you, Freya?" Soren's hand was still tangled in her hair, still pulling her head back.

Freya screamed again, like a wounded animal caught in a trap.

Devlin wanted her to be his sweet, gentle, kind Freya.

Soren wanted her naked on her knees, begging him to take her.

She couldn't please them both. She couldn't be both girls. Their conflicting desires were tearing her apart.

She fainted.

When she awoke, she was in her room and the house was in chaos.

There were angry voices shouting downstairs—men's voices.

Jadzia sat on the bed across from her.

"Mother told me to stay here with you so you don't do something stupid."

The waves of hate rolling off Jadzia were so strong that Freya almost opened the window and jumped.

"Don't," Jadzia said. "Mother very specifically told me that I'd be to blame if you somehow ended up dead."

"What happened?" Freya whispered.

Jadzia crossed her arms and leaned back against the wall.

"Well, Soren's dead and Devlin is being charged with

murder. Seems he didn't realize that his dear, sweet Freya was willing to spread her legs for anyone who asked."

"What?" Freya sat up, looking towards the door.

"You heard me." Jadzia moved to stand between Freya and the door. "Seems Devlin saw Soren with his pants down around his ankles and heard you scream and got the wrong impression. So, he killed him. But when Britt found out about it, he told everyone how you were nothing but a no good, dirty little tramp. And then a whole lot of other men backed him up. Told stories about coming here while we were all in town and paying to be with you."

Jadzia sneered down at her. "Not that the money was needed, of course. They all made it pretty clear you'd be just as willing to open your legs for free. Now Devlin is going to be hanged because he was in love with a no good dirty whore."

"No. You don't understand…" Freya reached toward Jadzia, but her sister stepped out of her reach.

"You disgust me. You *should* die."

With that, Jadzia left her alone.

Soren had deserved to die for what he'd done to her.

But Devlin…Devlin didn't deserve any of this.

Freya should've turned Devlin away after what had happened at the river.

She wasn't worthy of him. But she couldn't. Because he'd still wanted her.

He hadn't known what she'd become. And it wouldn't matter now even if she told him the truth.

She'd done it, hadn't she? She'd kept seeing the men and hiding it from her mother.

Freya could've told someone. After the men had left. When she was herself once more.

But she hadn't.

Not that anyone would have wanted to hear it.

Not her mother. And certainly not Devlin.

They'd wanted her to be their old Freya. The sweet child who skipped and sang silly songs.

But she wasn't that girl anymore.

And she never would be again.

Freya snuck out the back of the house and sprinted toward the Mill Bridge. This had started in the river, let it end in the river.

She ran to the middle of the bridge, ready to fling herself over the railing. But at the sight of the swirling waters below, she hesitated.

Death was so final.

But did she have any other choice?

She couldn't face them. Couldn't stand to see the look of betrayal in Devlin's eyes. The hatred and disgust in her father's. And without them, she had nowhere left to go.

She braced herself to jump, but, as she leaned forward, she no longer had the will for it.

She would've sighed in regret, but she couldn't, because she was no longer alone.

"Child, what are you doing?" The man who spoke to her was middle-aged, his clothes covered in dust, his eyes kind.

"I was going to jump. I wanted to die."

He chuckled. "Well, that's the most honest response I've ever received to that question."

"You wanted an honest response, so I gave you one."

"I see." He studied her for a moment more before continuing. "Come here, child."

Freya obeyed.

"That was easy."

"I didn't have a choice. I had to obey you. But as soon as you leave me alone, I'll go back and jump."

"I see…" He looked around. "Where are your people?"

"I have no people. Not anymore."

"Ah. Well then. I guess you'll just have to come along with me. Can't have pretty young ladies jumping off of bridges under my watch. I'm Brandon. And you are?"

"Freya."

"Nice to meet you, Freya. Now come along."

Brandon walked away, Freya trailing him.

"So, young lady, tell me about yourself. How did you come to stand on that bridge?"

Freya told him. About the blueberries, the river, the hunter, Hakan, Soren, Devlin. All of it. Brandon listened, his brow creased in concern, arms clasped behind his back.

Freya expected to feel that pull from him that she'd felt from the other men, but she didn't.

He didn't want her, not like they had. He didn't want her weak and subject to his will.

He wanted her to be safe and strong.

To be herself.

Somewhere deep inside a tiny flicker of will blossomed and she could feel Brandon supporting her, anchoring her. "How did you do that?"

He winked. "Give it time, child. It will get better. I promise."

Freya smiled for the first time since that day by the river as she walked by his side, protected by his belief in her, finally free to be herself for the first time in weeks.

She allowed herself to believe.

That maybe there was a way to live with "it". A way to be strong, to be herself again. To feel the desires of others, but to resist them.

To choose for herself what she did and when.

THE BEARER

I try not to shiver as I stand in the center of the exam room, my belly exposed to the cool air. The lights are always a little too white, bleaching everything of color, banishing the shadows. I glance at the plush sofa along the wall, longing to sit down, but knowing that I have to stand here for as long as it takes.

I practice my breathing exercises, finding the calm center within, and I wait.

Finally, the other door opens and two women enter. One is Doctor Benford. We've never been introduced, but that's what the nurses call her. She's older and she never smiles, but she always seems kind.

The other woman appears young. It's hard to tell what her real age might be with the work she's had done. Everything about her is tight—all hard lines and angles.

There's no softness. Not in her face or her eyes. And not in the hands that touch me.

I stare straight ahead as she kneels down in front of me and runs her fingers along my flesh, following the curve of my belly as she waits for a response from the child I carry inside.

Her hands are cold where they touch my skin, and I struggle not to flinch away from her.

This is the third time she's been here to check on the child. Like I'll somehow fail if she doesn't.

I've heard stories of Mothers who visit frequently, in awe of the child growing inside their Bearer. Women who marvel and coo and smile in pure bliss at the thought of the child they'll soon hold in their arms.

My Mother is not like that.

"You've been giving her the fenurine-enriched food?" she asks Doctor Benford.

"Yes, per your request. But I should remind you that the long-term studies show that fenurine-enriched foods adversely affect the Bearer's health." The doctor responds without looking at me, her attention focused on the Mother.

Shrugging, the Mother rises. "My interest is in giving my child the best possible opportunity. Will the fenurine affect the Bearer's health in the next five months?"

"No. But..."

"Then what's the problem?" The Mother raises one perfectly sculpted brow in question, stick-thin arms crossed, toe pointed forward like a dagger.

"Well, the fenurine is an added cost and, even though it won't affect this pregnancy, it may affect the Bearer's future pregnancies..."

The Mother smiles a thin-lipped smile. "Money. Of course that's the issue. Discuss it with Scott. I'm sure the two of you can determine a reasonable fee to compensate for the inconvenience."

"I'm so sorry to have brought it up. I really do hate discussing money matters with respect to such a joyous event."

The Mother laughs—a cold, barking sound.

"Joyous? Please. I'm having a child because I need to have a child. I fully intend to enroll it in your infant development program once it's born. Save that 'joyous' clap-trap for your throwback types that would 'have a child themselves if only they could'."

She walks out the door, the doctor following behind, neither one glancing back at me.

As the door closes, I hear her continue, "I've been reading some promising studies about in utero motor skill development..."

After they leave, I stroke the curve of my belly, crooning softly to the child I carry inside. I feel her fluttering movements and smile. My sweet Kiukiu is so strong.

"You know you're not supposed to do that," Nurse Helen says. I startle at the sound of her voice, blushing, and stop humming. But I continue to stroke my belly while she unties my shirt.

"What if the mother came back in and heard you? She'd have a fit. And if anything turned out to be wrong with the baby, she'd blame it on us for 'failing to maintain the appropriate environment'."

I nod, casting my eyes down at the floor, studying the cracks in the tiles. Nurse Helen is right. But the thought of Kiukiu growing inside me with only the sounds of her Mother's voice and classical music makes me sad. I want her to know that someone loves her.

Even if it is just her Bearer.

I wish Nurse Helen understood the hand signals my aunt taught me, but none of the nurses do. Not anymore.

Unable to communicate, I stare at the floor and wait.

"Come along. Just because the mother visits doesn't mean you can skip your routine..."

A week later, I stand once more under the harsh white lights while the Mother runs her hands along my belly. Her nails are just long enough to scratch against my skin.

Kiukiu pokes a foot out at the touch, tracing a long line across my belly.

"Excellent. It seems to be progressing nicely. Scott, do you want to touch it?"

Scott. The Father.

He's the first man I've ever seen in person. I tried to ignore him, to stare at the wall and focus on my breathing, but I couldn't help but steal glances at him while the Mother examined me.

Now he stands and approaches, smiling slightly as I accidentally meet his gaze. I notice how the corner of his eyes crinkle and I feel a warmth spread through my body, banishing the cold of the room.

He coughs nervously, slowing to a shuffle as he comes closer.

"Really, Scott? It's not a big deal." The Mother frowns at him as she walks over to the doctor, leaving us alone.

"Hello there. I'm Scott." He tries to make eye contact, but I continue to study the cracks in the floor, swallowing. My cheeks feel hot and it's suddenly hard to breathe. I want to leave, but I can't.

"Scott, what are you doing? You don't introduce yourself to them."

The Mother shakes her head in annoyance before turning back to the doctor. The Father, Scott, makes a funny face at me. I almost laugh before I stop myself.

Doctor Benford turns to watch us. "Mr. Baker, our Bearers are very well trained. In fact, it's better if you don't engage with them. In order to maintain the mother's primary bond with the child, our Bearers remain silent for the duration of the pregnancy. Please, just go ahead and interact with your child."

Doctor Benford and the Mother move over to the corner of the room and start discussing a scan, their heads close together.

The Father kneels down in front of me. I focus my gaze on the wall behind him, trying not to think about how close he is. I can feel the heat radiating from his body, smell the spiciness of his scent, hear the quiet exhalation of his breath.

He reaches out, and I close my eyes, bracing for his fingers on my skin. But I feel nothing. Opening my eyes once more, I see him blowing softly on his hands.

He sees my confusion and smiles. "Don't want cold hands on your belly now, do we?"

Before I can stop myself, I smile.

He places his hands on my belly, his eyes still on mine, and I feel a shiver up my spine. His touch is like warm honey. Neither one of us are smiling now as his hands move along the curve of my skin in slow, gentle strokes.

I want to look away, but I can't.

I know I'm nothing to him. Just his Bearer. Nothing more.

But I can't look away. And I don't want him to stop.

I imagine reaching a hand down to stroke his head in the same way he's stroking my belly, my fingers running through his hair as he stares up at me with adoring eyes and that little hint of a smile on his lips...

Kiukiu chooses that moment to poke one lazy little elbow into his hand and his eyes light up with joy. His mouth opens in an "o" of surprise as he looks down and gently runs a finger along the little bump. I watch them interact, adoring them both.

The Mother interrupts us. "Scott, it's time to go. We have that three o'clock in infant development."

He grimaces and slowly rises to his feet.

As his wife and the doctor leave, he turns back and reaches a hand to tuck a piece of hair behind my ear, his fingers lingering.

"Take care of her for me, okay?" He smiles at me once more before following them.

After he leaves, I put my hand to my face, remembering the soft brush of his fingertips.

I'm still staring at the door when Nurse Helen comes to lead me away.

The next day, I feel shaky, disjointed. My hands tremble as I try to eat breakfast and I push away the bowl of optimally balanced nutrients ideal for a pregnant woman.

"Ka? Are you okay? You need to finish your breakfast."

I shake my head, grimacing in disgust at the thought of eating another bite.

"Ka? I know it doesn't taste very good, but it's the best possible food for the baby. And you need to eat all of it."

I know from my aunt's stories that if I refuse to eat the food they'll feed me intravenously. While I'm a Bearer my body is not my own. They'll do whatever they need for the baby.

Sighing, I pull the bowl back. Using one hand to pinch my nose closed, I manage to gulp down the remainder of the meal, resisting the urge to run to the bathroom and throw it back up.

I blame it on lack of sleep, but I'm wrong.

In yoga class I can't find the rhythm. I'm used to losing myself in the flow of the poses, in the pattern of the breath. But today my thoughts are of him. Of the Father.

I remember the warmth of his hands as they moved along my belly, the way his fingers stroked the side of my face. I see his smile. I smell him. Hear the way his voice vibrated as he introduced himself.

I try to hold the Tree Pose, but stumble, falling to the side.

"Ka? Are you okay? Perhaps you should see the doctor."

They send me for tests—blood, urine, heart rate, vision. While they're poking and prodding me, I listen to the steady drone of the Mother's voice rising from the speakers pressed against my belly.

"Hello there little one. I'm your mother..." Her voice is wooden, cold.

I imagine what one of those cooing Mothers would sound like, her voice rising and falling, full of warmth and love transmitted through sound from the speakers to the little one I carry inside.

But that's not my Mother. For her, reading the script was just one more item on the to-do list. *Read soothing script for unborn fetus.* Check. Done. Over.

They talk in hushed tones about the effects of the fenurine, but I know that's not what caused me to lose my balance.

It was him. The Father.

Three days later, I once again stand in the center of the room, belly exposed to the cold air, the lights so bright they hurt. I try to wait patiently, to find my centering breath, but I'm tired. My legs shake uncontrollably. Little tremors I hope they won't notice.

At last, *he* walks through the door, flashing the smile I've seen every night in my dreams.

My cheeks hurt with the fierceness of my return smile before I remember what I am and once again focus my gaze on the floor tiles, tracing the cracks in the third tile from the door.

They look like a bird if I squint just right.

He turns to Doctor Benford. "I'd like to be alone with my child if you don't mind."

"Of course, Mr. Baker. Please press the red button by the door if you need anything."

"I will."

I hear the door click closed and look up to see him leaning his weight against it, arms crossed, watching me. He's frowning slightly and I wonder what I've done wrong.

I shiver, the little tremors in my legs moving through my body in a wave I can't control.

"Are you okay? Here. Come sit on the couch. Your feet must be killing you."

He guides me to the couch. I tense, unable to move. He's so close I can smell a mustiness to him and see small beads of sweat on his brow.

"Better?" He peers into my eyes and smooths my hair back from my face.

I nod, refusing to look at him, rubbing my arms against the chill.

"Here." He takes off his jacket and drapes it around my shoulders. "Can't have my Bearer freeze to death, now can I?" he asks.

I risk looking at him, but look away quickly when our eyes meet.

"You know I'd never given much thought to you before the other day. Bearers, I mean. Not you. Well, I guess you, too. I'd just never thought…"

He trails off, staring at the far wall. I watch him stand and pace the room, running his hands through his short hair. I want to help, but I don't know what to do, so I sit there shivering, pulling his coat closer to my body.

"What's your name?" he asks, turning around suddenly in the midst of his circuit.

I shake my head, reminding him I'm not allowed to talk.

"It's okay, I don't mind if you talk." He sits down in front of me and takes my hands in his. "I want to know about you. You are carrying my child after all."

He says this last with a sort of half-smile and I look away, chewing on my lip like I used to when I was a child.

I stare at our hands together, dark against light; move my palm so it's touching his, see how much smaller mine is. Our fingers interlace for a moment before he snatches his hand back.

When I look up at him, unsure what's wrong, he's staring at me intensely.

"I shouldn't have come here. I'm sorry." He drops my hands and leaves, never looking back.

The door closes firmly behind him and I move to it, placing my hand against the smooth surface. His coat hangs heavy on my shoulders.

I wish for him to return, but he doesn't.

When Nurse Helen enters a few moments later, I'm still standing there. She tsks, shaking her head at something I don't understand.

She takes the jacket from my shoulders and I shiver violently as the cold air assaults me.

"Ka? Are you okay? I'm going to get Doctor Benford. Sit down."

She leads me over to the hard metal table in the corner and leaves me there, waiting for the doctor.

That night, as I stare at the wall waiting for sleep to come, tears roll down my face and soak the pillow. I don't know why I'm crying; I've been told pregnancy does that to you sometimes.

I wish my aunt was here.

She'd know what to do—what's wrong with me.

I miss her and all the late nights we spent playing cards and practicing silence.

I remember her telling me once, when she'd had a little too much fermented coconut milk and her eyes had taken on that far away look, "No one else will understand what you feel. No one other than a Bearer will understand your loss."

I think in that moment that I understand what she meant.

I'm wrong.

Almost two weeks pass before I see him again.

Nurse Helen wheels me into the room and helps me onto the cold slab of metal. It's early spring but I'm wearing a thick wrap to keep away the cold. The shakes in my legs are so bad that I can't walk more than a few feet at a time.

My aunt never told me it would be like *this*.

He trails along behind the Mother and Doctor Benford, hanging back, his hands moving restlessly as he crosses and uncrosses his arms.

When he sees me lying there, shivering against the cold, he surges towards me before stopping himself with a furtive glance at his wife.

I know I should look away. I'm just an object, a thing to them. The only reason I'm there is because the baby can't be there without me.

But I can't.

The sight of him steadies me.

A small tear falls down my cheek. I ignore it, too scared to wipe it away as the Mother and doctor approach.

"We'd like to wean her off the fenurine."

"Why? Every study I've read says that fenurine, if used during pregnancy, gives babies advanced motor skills."

"I understand that, but the effect it's having on the Bearer ..."

"I don't care about the Bearer. I care about the baby. Is it having an effect on the baby?"

I turn my head towards the wall, not wanting to listen. Not wanting to hear more.

A hand strokes my hair and I smell the crisp scent of soap. I know without looking that it's him. Who else would it be?

I close my eyes and cling to the sensation of his fingers in my hair while the women poke and prod me.

They continue to discuss the fenurine, the doctor unable to articulate a reason to stop it, the Mother adamant that it continue.

All I care about is him. Nothing else matters in that moment.

I'm not sure how long it lasts, but they finally leave me alone, curled on the cold metal table, to wait for Nurse Helen.

The next day, the Father returns alone.

He's angry. Agitated. He never sits, just paces furiously back and forth.

I watch, shaking against a chill that no amount of layers can touch.

"It's not supposed to be like this is it?" he asks, turning to me.

I shake my head. Shrug.

"Damn it. These ridiculous rules. Well, I don't give a damn about their rules. I'm the father of this child and I say you can talk. So, talk to me. Is this normal?"

I shrink back from the anger in his voice, but I answer. "No. I-I don't think so."

"Is this your first child?"

I nod, biting my lip.

"Then how would you know?"

"My family…my mother, my aunt, my grandmother…they were all Bearers."

"And none had a pregnancy like this?"

"I don't think so."

He kneels down in front of me and takes my hands. "What about the baby?"

"Kiukiu?"

"Kiukiu?" He responds, puzzled.

I blush and look away. "That's what I call her."

"Does it mean something?"

I nod again, scared to tell him. I don't know why. He's been so nice to me. But this is mine. The little piece of her that I'll get to keep even after they've taken her away.

"*What* does it mean?" He laughs, a short little sound. "You know, I don't even know *your* name. What is it?"

Now I really blush.

"Ka. My name is Ka. And Kiukiu means precious."

"And what does Ka mean?" His eyes sparkle. "Beautiful? Beloved?"

I shake my head and refuse to answer, not wanting to share my shame with him. Fortunately, he doesn't have a chance to ask again, because at that moment I start to shake so hard I can't speak.

"Ka! Ka? Look at me. Nurse!"

He pulls me into his arms, shouting for a nurse until one finally arrives.

The next few hours are a blur.

Once again, I find myself lying on a cold table, my eyes closed against the bright lights as doctors and nurses swarm around me. They give me something that makes me feel all warm and floaty, like I'm on a giant ocean of yellow clouds.

I know he's still there. I can hear him shouting, demanding that they tell him what's happening.

They try to calm him, letting him know that the baby is unaffected and that it should survive.

"I don't give a damn about the baby. What about Ka?" he screams before I float away.

When I finally awake, the lights are dim and there are tubes snaking from my arms to various bags and machines. The first thing I do is reach for my belly, but my arms are tethered to the sides of the bed and I whimper in fear.

He's there, stroking my hair, squeezing my hand. "It's okay, Ka. I'm here."

"Kiukiu?"

"She's fine. It was a little scary there for a bit, but you should both be safe now. They've taken you off the fenurine."

"But...the Mother..."

He smiles. Not the warm crinkly smile, but a sad, determined smile. "She'll get over it."

I shake my head. "No. I'll take the fenurine. For Kiukiu. It's what will make her the best."

"No, Ka. I won't allow it."

I try to protest further, but he reaches across the bed and pushes a button and I feel the yellow haze rise up to swallow me once more.

"Sleep. Get better," he whispers, kissing my forehead.

The next time I awake, I'm back in my own room. It's dark and I'm alone.

I lie there, singing softly to Kiukiu and stroking my belly, feeling her small flutters of movement. She loves to hear me sing.

I think about calling a nurse, but I'm too tired to move.

I restart my routine the next day—yoga, musical play, and Mother recordings every hour. I try to ignore the harsh grating sound of her voice as it drifts from the speakers but it worms its way under my skin like an itch I can't scratch.

I wish there were Father recordings. I imagine the soft sound of *his* voice surrounding me, full of love and compassion. I imagine they're for me *and* the child I carry inside.

Things seem normal, but I know they're not. The nurses whisper when they see me, faces sad or thoughtful. I try to get Nurse Helen to tell me what's wrong, but she just shakes her head.

"Behave as if nothing happened, Ka. They may still bring

her around. And if they do, we want her to know that all of the protocols were followed in the interim."

I don't understand. But I do as I'm told.

He doesn't return.

Neither does the Mother.

I live my days in a haze of routine, but I think about him always. I wonder what happened; why the Mother no longer comes to inspect her child.

Then one day I feel a sharp pain and know it's time. It's too early, but it's time.

They take me to another cold room with bright lights where too many people huddle around me, shouting instructions.

"Push, Ka, push...Okay, good girl, now rest...Ready to push again? All right, here we go..."

On and on it goes. Hours crawl by in a blur of pain and weariness until finally, when they've started to talk about cutting me open—something a Bearer never wants—my little Kiukiu is born.

She's small, barely the size of Doctor Benford's hand, and she gives a sad little mewl of sound instead of the lusty scream I'd been told to expect. But she's there. And she's alive.

I see the looks of concern as the nurses glance at one another. Doctor Benford shakes her head.

"What is it? What's wrong?" I ask Nurse Helen, grasping for her arm, finally allowed to speak after all these months.

"It's nothing, Ka. Just lie back. You still need to deliver the afterbirth." She pushes me down, her hands gentle but firm.

"No...Tell me what's wrong."

"Later. I promise. Right now, we need you to finish with the delivery."

They carry Kiukiu from the room while Nurse Helen holds me down, gently but firmly.

They drug me. I don't wake up until the next day.

No one will tell me what happened to her.

They say it's not my concern. I'm a Bearer. I bore the child. It was the end of my involvement. She's someone else's now.

He comes to see me the next day.

"Scott!" I say, unable to hide my excitement.

"Ka. How are you?" He tries to smile, but fails.

"What's wrong?" I ask, suddenly scared.

All of the nurses' looks, the Mother's absence, his absence. It all starts to come together in my mind. "How's Kiukiu? You've seen her haven't you?"

"No, Ka. I haven't. She was…she was deemed unsatisfactory. Premature. Below approved birth weight."

"No." I start to cry.

"It wasn't your fault, Ka. The doctors think it was a result of the fenurine. You can still be a Bearer."

I look at him for a moment, trying to understand.

I don't care about being a Bearer. I care about Kiukiu, the child I carried inside for seven months.

But he's right. I've heard the stories. Of other Bearers. Unable to carry a child to term or bear satisfactory children for their Mothers and Fathers. Bearers rejected by their families and turned out on the streets—alone and starving with no skills other than the ability to be silent.

I've heard worse.

What choice does a woman have when she has nothing but her body?

I've heard the stories, but never thought they could happen to me.

I try to sit up. "Where is Kiukiu?"

"She's gone, Ka. I'm sorry."

"Gone? Where?"

He doesn't answer me, just shakes his head and won't meet my eyes.

I really cry then and he holds me close as my tears soak his shirt. He strokes my back like he once stroked my belly, but his touch no longer feels like warm honey.

He stays for a time, talking about his life, tells me a funny story about a dog he once owned. I try to listen, try to laugh like I know he wants, but all I can think of is Kiukiu.

A nurse stands in the doorway. She doesn't say anything, but I know she's there to take him away.

"Give me a moment," he says, dismissing her.

He turns back to me and I see such a mix of emotions on his face that I can't capture even one of them. He smiles softly, taking my hand in his. "You never told me what Ka stands for."

He says it like it's some special treat I've been keeping from him.

I hate him in that moment.

For not keeping Kiukiu and for making me reveal my shame.

"Two," I say.

"Two what?"

"Ka. Two. I was the second daughter, so they named me Ka."

"They named you Two?" He stares at me in horror.

I nod, my face red with shame and eyes full of tears.

"How old are you?" he asks, as if it suddenly occurred to him to wonder.

"Sixteen."

He stiffens, his hand squeezing mine too tight.

"Sixteen? I thought…I thought you had to be older to…"

"Most Bearers don't start until they're seventeen. But my sister, Jun, was caught with a boy and thrown out. She couldn't come. And we needed the money."

I try not to think of that day. Try not to remember her screams as they dragged her away.

A Bearer must be pure, untouched. She was unclean, so unwanted. They put her out like so much trash and sent me to take her place.

Scott leans close, trying to meet my gaze. "They sent you here when you were fifteen?"

"Yes." I shrug. "I was capable of Bearing. Why not?" My father's debts couldn't wait.

"I didn't think …"

"No, you didn't." I snap at him. The first time I've snapped at anyone. Ever.

The fire of my anger burns in my belly, raw and white hot. All consuming. I want to lash out. At someone, anyone, for what happened to me.

And to Kiukiu.

"Ka, I'm sorry."

I ignore him. I want him gone.

The nurse comes by again. "Mr. Baker. I really do have to insist that you leave now. Ka needs to rest. It was most unusual to let you see your Bearer after the birth and…"

"Yes, yes. I know. Just give me another minute."

The nurse hesitates, but finally leaves once more.

"Ka, I am so sorry. I had no idea. I...here." He hands me a slip of paper. It has writing on it, but I can't read so I don't know what it says.

"If you ever need me, you can contact me. Okay? Just call this number here and they'll find me."

I look at the card. Part of me, this new angry part, wants to tear the useless piece of paper into little pieces and throw it back in his face. What does he care, really? He's going to walk out that door and go back to his life as if nothing happened.

As if Kiukiu never even existed.

But another part of me clutches the card close. It's a sliver of hope—that someday maybe I can have a different life. A life that doesn't depend on my ability to bear children and stay silent.

I force myself to thank him, tucking the card away where the nurses won't find it.

He gently kisses me on the forehead before he stands to leave.

In the doorway he pauses. "Ka, why don't you choose your own name? Just because someone named you Two doesn't mean you have to keep it."

He's right. But what name would I choose? Two is as good a name as any.

I shake my head. "Ka is who I am."

"No. No, it's not."

I flinch from the anger in his voice and his clenched fists.

He looks at me for a moment and narrows his eyes in thought. "How do you say butterfly?"

I stare at him. After all of this, he thinks me a butterfly? Something fragile and vulnerable that flits from here to there? Pretty, but nothing more?

Of course he does.

They all do.

But no. That is not who I am. Not now. Not even for this man whose first touch was like warm honey awakening me from my dream.

"Well?" He smiles at me.

"Ah-toc-la," I say. "If I call you, that's the name I'll use. Ah-toc-la."

"Atocla." He frowns slightly, knowing somehow that it isn't the pretty little name for me. He nods slightly. "Atocla. It suits you."

It does. Because from now on I won't be some nameless, voiceless body they can use for their own purposes. From this day forward I will be Atocla. She who brings the fire.

I'll see them burn.

For Kiukiu.

And for myself.

THE PRICE WE PAY

Clark lay in bed, eyes squeezed tight.

"God, give me the strength to face another day," he prayed, steeling himself.

He wondered what it must be like for other people to wake up—how did it feel to just live instead of having to claw back every single hour from the hands of the Reaper? He believed in God, but Death was like a close personal friend who had come to crash on the couch for a few days and never left.

He moved carefully as he rose, trying not to wince at the sharp stabs of pain that shot through his shoulder where the bones were slowly decaying—long-term victims of the disease that had already stolen his kidneys.

Molly was still asleep, one arm thrown above her head, long hair sprawled on the pillow.

He stood there, slightly hunched, frail in his white under-wear, and wondered what he'd done to deserve such a remark-able woman.

And whether he'd be able to keep her.

They'd had two kids and fifteen years together already. But they'd also spent countless nights in the hospital and too many days worrying whether they'd have enough social credits for the next dialysis treatment.

How much could love overcome? When would she finally say enough and leave him?

He wouldn't blame her if she did.

Sometimes he secretly hoped she would.

He'd die if she left—inside if not outside—but he hated how their love kept her here, suffering along with him.

He'd wanted to give her the world once.

Instead he'd given her this cramped existence—constantly on the brink of failure, never able to just live.

She woke and saw him watching her.

"Come back to bed. You can be a few hours late, can't you?" Her voice was soft and low, still fuzzy with sleep.

He wanted to so badly, but, no. He couldn't be late again. His boss would surely fire him this time.

"I can't."

"At least give me a kiss." She smiled, the familiar fire burning in her eyes.

He shook his head. If he gave her one kiss it would become two and then he *would* be a few hours late. And if he lost this job…

No. He had plans. Simple ones, but ones that mattered. Like taking the family to the mountains for a week.

He'd have enough if he could just keep this job another two months, which was easier said than done. It was his third job so far this year. He tried to keep his head down and do what he was told, but it was hard when he could so easily see what his bosses couldn't.

But he'd do it this time. For Molly and the kids.

It would be worth it to see the smile on Molly's face when he surprised her with the trip.

For now, though...The light in Molly's eyes died and she turned away, burying her face in the pillow.

Clark paused a moment, wanting to comfort her, but he didn't have time. He never did.

He turned towards the bathroom, promising himself he'd buy her a rose on the way home from work. That much he could afford, at least.

Clark tried not to look in the mirror as he brushed his teeth. Tried not to register the gaunt frame and loose skin where once there'd been taut flesh and muscle.

At least the worst scar was in the back—the jagged line along his shoulder blade where they'd removed his lung after the second and final failed kidney transplant.

That one had almost cost him his life. The Reaper had decided to not just crash on the couch and play video games, but had slept in his bed, worn his clothes, and eaten all his food.

Three months he'd been in the hospital. He'd spent endless days with green and black infection spewing from his mouth; weeks of fighting until they finally acknowledged that it was no good to save the kidney if the patient was dead.

He'd spent those months tethered to a hospital bed watching Molly hide her tears, pretending for his sake that everything was fine.

He'd done the same for her—not let her see how close Death was and how much just opening his eyes every morning was a struggle.

He would have never made it without her love to light the way.

And every day they'd had to wonder if this would be the day the hospital stopped treatment. The day he finally ran out of social credits and they decided he was no longer valuable enough to society to save and shut down the machines keeping him alive.

Every morning he'd wondered if that would be the last time he'd look into Molly's warm brown eyes.

It had taken him three long years to save enough credits for that surgery. Hundreds of hours keeping his head down, doing what he was told, keeping silent lest he be fired. And when he wasn't working, he was volunteering. He'd tutored students, cleaned-up parks, done taxes for seniors—anything to earn another credit.

Three years of sacrifice so he could finally live a normal life.

He and Molly had lain together at night whispering about what they could do when he was healthy again—travel anywhere they wanted for as long as they wanted, stay in bed all day on a Saturday instead of rushing off to dialysis.

Eat a banana split together.

Three years they'd spent dreaming about what it would be like after.

After.

It was all they'd lived for.

Not that they would have ever been completely free.

Clark would have always been on anti-rejection medicines. Not to mention that if he'd ever rejected the kidney he'd have needed enough social credits for the surgery to remove the failed kidney and go back on dialysis.

But it would have been a *better* life. A more normal life.

Especially better than the years when he'd been so low on credits that Molly had been forced to dialyze him at home using that old brown monstrosity that barely functioned.

After, he'd told her as he stroked her hair. *After the transplant, it will all be better.*

How wrong he'd been.

Clark shoved thoughts of what could have been to the back of his mind. Dwelling on the past did nothing for his present.

He opened the blister pack of his morning medications and swallowed the fifteen pills one at a time, hating each one as he washed it down with a sip of tepid tap water. He had to take half of them just to counteract the side effects of the others. It was a never-ending death spiral that he'd lose some day. Only question was when.

Sometimes he wished he weren't a thinking man. That he could just walk through life like some mindless drone, oblivious to what was happening around and to him.

But he wasn't. He saw it all. The unfairness, the futility.

When it all became too much he did multiplication tables in his head—32 x 43, 45 x 87, 921 x 435. Anything to distract himself from the reality of his life and the anger at those who put such a low value on their fellow man.

Otherwise he'd start calculating how he could steal enough supplies to treat himself for a year. And wonder what it would take to overthrow a government that only allowed him medical treatment after he'd proven his continued value to society.

Such a joke.

They wanted him to prove his value but at the same time they chained him with their requirements.

If they had just given him the care he needed to survive, he'd have given them everything. Who knows where the world would be now if he'd been able to finish his PhD in nuclear physics? But no. He'd had to drop out when he turned twenty-five and they started demanding credits for his treatment.

He could have accomplished so much…

Instead he was stuck working part-time jobs, scrabbling and scratching just to get by.

He flung the blister pack at the trash can. He didn't have time for this shit.

Dwelling on the injustices of the world wasn't going to get him to work on time or keep the spark in Molly's eyes. Leave that to some idealist with good health and money in the bank. Someone with the time and energy to save the world. He didn't have either.

He glared at the broken man in the mirror and forced his shoulders back and lifted his chin. Time to face another day.

Clark paused in the doorway to the dining room, watching his daughter and son eat their breakfast, one fair, one dark, both intent on last-minute homework as they ate the nutritional slop provided by the local foodbank.

They were what made it all worthwhile. They were why he could swallow his pride every morning and do what had to be done.

"Daddy!" Bella ran over to him, her hair shining white under the glare of the lights. "Can I come to work with you today?"

"No, Munchkin, sorry. You have to go to school." He ruffled her hair.

She pouted, big brown eyes pleading with him.

"And I'm in the office all day. You know you can't come into the office with me."

Her shoulders slumped and she shuffled back to the table. "Fine."

Seven years old and he already worried about her. So feisty and independent. How would a girl like her survive in a world that determined whether she could live based upon some narrow pre-conceived notion of social value much less thrive?

He was afraid someday she'd be standing at the front of a mob screaming for change, unable to bow her head the way he had all these years. Maybe that was a good thing…The world needed to change. But did it have to do so on the back of his daughter?

As he sat down, he turned to Drake who was hunched over his food, his dark hair flopped over his eyes. He was so angry these days—twelve years old and he'd finally started to understand how the world really worked—you either had enough money and could do whatever you wanted or you spent your days playing their game, racking up social credits against your inevitable need.

"How're you doing, Buddy? Ready for the game this weekend?"

Drake shrugged. "I guess. Probably won't start."

"Well, you'll still earn participation points even if you don't."

"I don't care about participation points! I didn't go out for the stupid team for participation points. I went out because I wanted to play." Drake glared into his bowl.

"I know. But participation points matter, so it's good that you're earning them."

Some weeks the few credits Clark received from his kids' participation points made the difference between receiving treatment and not.

Clark's vision went white.

He fought the urge to hit something. No point in hating the world for the way it was. It didn't hate him back. It just was.

"Maybe we can go to the court this weekend and work on your hook shot. What do you say?" Clark watched his son, wishing Drake would look at him.

Drake glared into his bowl. "You'll probably be too tired."

Clark winced. He *was* often tired on the weekends. Dialysis took it out of him. And that on top of work and volunteering and trying to be a good husband and father.

He tried, but each year he lost a little more ground to the Reaper.

"No. I won't. We'll go on Sunday. After church."

Drake rolled his eyes, but was too smart to say anything against going to church.

Bella moved the gray sludge around in her bowl, lower lip thrust out and tears lurking in the corners of her eyes.

"You want to come with us this weekend, Munchkin?"

She bobbed her head. "Yes! And, Daddy?"

"Yeah?"

"Can I go to dialysis with you tomorrow?"

He'd been planning on banking some more social credits while he dialyzed—completing some government questionnaire or other—but he couldn't say no to her twice. He'd just have to find some other time to answer the questionnaire.

"Of course, Munchkin."

"Thank you, Daddy." She leaned over and kissed him on the cheek before running to her room to get ready for school.

He watched her go, fighting the urge to give up and go back to bed right then. Some days it was all just too much.

Bella going to dialysis with him meant he needed to visit Joe today. She didn't need to see that. And she was getting old enough to put two and two together and he didn't want to have that conversation with her just yet.

Because Joe had decided he was done. No more dialysis. After spending every Saturday morning for the last decade strapped to a machine next to Clark, Joe had decided it was time to call it quits. To die.

Most patients crammed into the public ward brought their own personal immersion units and spent the three hours lost in an alternate reality, but not Clark and Joe. They passed the time playing a game of chess or two on Clark's old wooden set. Or, more often than not, debating the latest psychology research. (Joe was a professor at the local university.)

They were partners in tragedy. Clark had lost his kidneys to a perfectly preventable childhood illness that wasn't caught in time, but Joe's story was even more unfortunate. He'd donated a kidney to his sister when he was in his twenties and then lost the other to an infection picked up while traveling South America on an aid mission thirty years later. He'd refused to even consider a kidney transplant, saying it was too much hassle for too little return.

And now, it seemed, he'd decided dialysis was too.

Clark made his way through the maze of long, beige hospital hallway to the wing dedicated to hopeless cases. "End Care" they called it. A place where they provided just enough pain medication to protect the living from a true view of what it was like to die.

Not everyone in End Care was there because they wanted to be, but when your veins were full of morphine you didn't have much left to fight back.

He found it a bit ironic that the same system that wouldn't keep a man alive was willing to provide him such a comfortable end.

Not too comfortable, of course. That wouldn't be cost effective.

Joe was in a room with three other patients, their beds separated by thin privacy curtains with bright images of flowers just artificial enough to be disturbing—the petals too thin, the colors nothing seen in nature.

The man next to Joe's bed was coughing—the sound loud and wet, as if he was trying to expel his insides through his throat.

The combined smells of decay and disinfectant made Clark miss a step, but he fought back his horror and made his way to Joe's bed.

Joe stared at the ceiling, his lips pressed tightly together, his hands clenched into fists.

"Hey Joe, whadya know?" Clark sat down in the red plastic chair with faux wood armrests next to the bed.

Joe turned towards him with a wince. "Clark. You didn't have to come."

"Of course I did. You're my friend."

"I would've understood if you didn't." He rolled his eyes towards the man still coughing nearby. "But, thank you." He reached out a hand already swollen from the fluids pooling in his body.

Clark took it, squeezing gently as he struggled to hold back the tears.

He didn't cry often, but to see Joe give up like this—like he himself had imagined doing in his darkest hours—was too much.

"Why?" Clark asked, unable to elaborate further.

"I was tired. Tired of all of it." Joe stared at the ceiling once more. "But mostly tired of being alone."

Clark winced. Joe's wife Celeste had died the year before and he hadn't been the same since.

"You could've..."

"What? Found someone? Gone online and met a great, caring woman to spend my days with?"

Clark nodded.

"Would you? If Molly left you? Would you do that to another woman knowing what you know now?"

Clark looked away. "No." Given the chance to do it again, he'd turn and run. Molly's love and their children were all that had made his life worth living. But to see his illness slowly break her down little by little, to watch the woman he loved try to bear a burden that no one should have to bear…

No.

He'd never ask that of another woman knowing what he did now.

He'd been young and foolish when they met, unaware how much a terminal illness would weave itself through every waking moment of their lives. How it would carve away at what they shared, day after day, slowly eroding the strong foundation they'd built together.

Even though he couldn't bear the thought of losing Molly —they'd separated the year before and even though he knew he should let her go, he hadn't been able to—he would never do that again. If he lost her, he'd die, alone and miserable before putting another woman he loved through that kind of hell.

Not that he could imagine loving anyone but her.

He shook his head and sat back, joining Joe in staring at the ceiling as the machines beeped and whirred around them and the smell of the place seeped into his very pores.

He knew God didn't give you more than you could handle, but he sure came damned close sometimes.

"How long?" He finally asked, desperate to fill the silence with something other than his thoughts.

"I don't know." Joe pressed the button for more morphine. "A week maybe? Could be less. Could be more. I stayed home the first week, tidying up, until it got to be too much and I decided I wanted to be close to the good drugs."

They laughed, the forced laughter of men who'd spent too many years relying on pills to regulate their bodies—veterans who had long since learned that pills could only do so much and even the good pills didn't touch every kind of pain.

Once again they lapsed into silence until Joe reached towards the nightstand. "Clark, I need to tell you something before I forget." He grunted in frustration as the tubes snaking out of his arm pulled him up short. "Can you get that folder for me?"

Clark handed him a dark blue folder with the name of some law firm glinting in gold embossed letters under the fluorescent light.

Joe thumbed through the documents inside until he found what he was looking for and handed it to Clark. "Here. All yours."

Clark read the words three times before they finally sunk in.

I, Joe O'Donnell, do hereby bequeath my entire estate to Clark Jones.

Further down the page, after a lot of words about being of sound mind and body and the legal requirements of the state, he saw two numbers: 225 social credits and $2,454,364.22.

Clark stared at the second number.

$2,454,364.22.

He reread the document. Two more times. Just to be sure.

The next paragraph spelled it out. Two million, four hundred fifty-four thousand, three hundred sixty-four dollars and twenty-two cents.

"Joe ..." Clark didn't know what to say. Thank you seemed so inadequate.

It was enough to pay for treatments for a decade, maybe more.

Enough to change his life. To change Molly's life.

Joe was staring at the ceiling again, but a tear slid down his cheek and to the pillow. "It's from Celeste's life insurance settlement. I couldn't bring myself to touch it." He smiled at Clark, his eyes moist with sorrow. "Use it wisely, my friend. Take that beautiful wife of yours to the mountains. Fish with your boy. Play chess with your girl. Maybe even go back to school."

Clark crumpled the paper in his fist as a mixture of gratitude, shame, hatred, and love coursed through his veins. Hatred for a system that made his dying friend's sacrifice mean so much. Love for a man who was too good for this world.

"Thank you," he whispered. "But couldn't you ..."

"No. I chose this. I'm ready."

Clark wanted to argue, but he nodded. He owed Joe the right to make this choice. He smoothed the paper out on his knee, too overcome to look at Joe again. "I'll come back each day until...until the end."

"No." Joe's voice was sharp and hard. "You don't need to see this."

"But I can't leave you here alone like this...To..."

"Go, Clark. Live your life."

Clark reached for the faded leather briefcase at his feet. "One last game of chess before I do?"

"Sure." Joe sat up straighter. "But if I win I'm taking that back ..."

He said it with a smile to show he was kidding, but Clark clutched the paper to his chest. No. He wouldn't give it back.

Slowly, he relaxed his grip on the document and shoved it into the briefcase, removing the worn wooden chessboard that had once belonged to his dad.

He forced a smile. "Good thing I'm going to win then, isn't

it?" he managed to say. All the while his heart was racing, pounding in his chest.

He knew Joe didn't mean it. But still. To come so close to finally being able to provide for his family…

He couldn't lose. Not now.

Two hours later, Clark sat across the street from the hospital in a bar with a neon sign above the door with half the letters missing so it looked like it was called "in's vern".

The place was empty except for a too-cozy couple sitting in the back corner by the lone pool table.

He'd taken a seat at the far end of the bar from them and sat staring at the bowl of potato chips the bartender had plopped down in front of him. Had Joe indulged in all the foods he wasn't supposed to eat after he'd made his choice? Spent the last week at home in one long binge fest of french fries, bananas, and orange juice? Or better yet, bacon potato skins smothered in cheese and sour cream.

And salt. Salt on everything.

"What'll you have?" The bartender, a big burly guy with faded green tattoos on his forearms, braced his hands on the counter and glared at Clark. No freeloaders allowed, it seemed.

"Whatever you have on tap." Clark winced as the man turned away. His body would punish him for having it, but sometimes he just wanted to be normal.

A little hard to do with his fistula throbbing with every beat of his heart. He moved his hand to his lap to hide it.

What was he doing here? Why hadn't he gone home to Molly? Why hadn't he told her the good news as soon as he left Joe's hospital room?

She'd be worried, wondering where he was.

He never stayed out late. Never missed a meal with his family to hang with the guys. Time with Molly and the kids was too precious to squander on conversations about shitty bosses and sports teams.

Yet here he was.

Alone in a bar.

Thinking.

He stared once more at the piece of paper Joe had given him. It was a wrinkled mess.

Joe had assured him it was a copy, but Clark carefully smoothed it out. He'd won three games to two at the end, but just barely, and probably more because Joe took pity on him. He'd been too nervous to think, the number repeating over and over again in his head with each move.

$2,454,364.22.

It was going to change their lives.

He could quit his job and go back to school. Take Molly on the honeymoon she'd always wanted. *Fly* the kids to Space Center and let them ride the zero gravity plane.

He imagined how different their lives would be, how much better they'd be now.

The bartender slammed the beer down and it sloshed onto the bar, almost spilling on the paper. Clark jerked it away.

Maybe he should save the money. Keep it for days when it all became too much and he just wanted to call in sick to work and stay in bed making love to his wife. Or ditch out early to watch his son's basketball game.

As he took a sip of the beer, grimacing at the strong yeasty taste of it—he hadn't had a beer in close to a decade—he realized something.

He could fail now. He could fail and his family would still be okay. The money would protect them.

They didn't need him anymore.

As a matter of fact, with the money, they'd probably be better off without him. One little heart infection and there it would go. They'd be right back where they'd started.

He flinched away from the imagined disappointment in Molly's eyes. From having to tell her that they needed to use the money for yet another surgery, yet another hospital stay. That she couldn't have the beautiful dress or those heart-shaped earrings he'd always wanted to buy her.

He pushed the beer away as an even worse thought occurred to him.

What if Molly left him? She'd wanted to the year before. The only reason she hadn't was because they hadn't had the money for her to actually move out.

But now…

Now she could take the money and the kids and leave him. She could start a new life. With someone healthy and happy. With a man who could give her everything she deserved.

He crumpled the paper. He didn't want to lose Molly. Or his kids. And he wasn't sure he could keep going, keep fighting, if he didn't actually have to.

But it was only a matter of time, wasn't it?

No matter what he did, no matter how much money he had, Death wasn't going to leave him be. The hourglass of his life was running low, the sands falling through faster and faster with each passing day.

He stared into the beer until it was warm and the couple had left, thinking.

Always thinking.

Molly was already in bed when Clark finally came home. He stumbled in the dark, trying to undress without waking her.

"How was Joe?" Her voice was deeper than normal as she reached out to where he sat on the edge of the bed.

He choked back the tears. "Bad."

"You weren't there this whole time were you?"

He crawled under the covers and turned to face her, their bodies curved towards one another; light from the streetlamp outside drawing stripes across her skin.

"No. I went to a bar. I needed to think."

"Oh."

One word, but a world of hurt in it. The hurt of a woman who'd been by his side through so much and who he shut away without even thinking about it. No matter how many times she told him he didn't need to protect her, that she wasn't some fragile creature who needed to be sheltered, he always tried to keep her from the worst of it.

"I love you so much." He pulled her close and buried his head against her neck, inhaling the spicy cinnamon scent of her skin.

She tensed, but didn't pull away from him. He kissed her neck and caressed her body until she finally melted under his touch, finally let him pull her close and make love to her with a desperate need and tenderness.

These moments, alone with her, in the darkness of night, were what sustained him. He'd never experienced pure joy the way he had when she was in his arms, moving with him, chasing new heights of passion. She was his core, the source of his strength.

He needed her.

After, they lay entwined, her head pillowed on his chest as she drifted to sleep.

Clark lay awake staring at the ceiling, watching the lights shift as an occasional car passed by outside.

There was so much he wanted to give his family, but some days he had so little left to give them.

He pictured Joe, alone in a hospital bed. All that money and he'd just quit. Handed the keys to the Reaper and walked out the door with a "try not to destroy the place" called over his shoulder.

He hadn't been able to hold on. Hadn't *wanted* to hold on. Not alone and sick like he was.

Clark clenched his fists. He'd never do that. Never just quit.

Would he?

He shivered. He'd been pulling so hard for so long just to keep from falling, he didn't know how else to live.

And now all the resistance was gone.

He didn't *have* to get out of bed in the morning. He didn't have to get out of bed ever again.

He stared at the ceiling, thinking, always thinking, until dawn arrived.

Clark lay in bed, eyes squeezed tight, knowing it was time to get up and start another day.

So much had changed in twenty-four hours. The fear that had driven him was gone.

No more worrying that today he wouldn't have enough credits to dialyze. No more needing to swallow his pride to keep his job or ask for assistance when he fell short.

He could finally be his own man.

And yet, nothing had really changed, had it?

He'd agreed to go three out of five against the Reaper and it was the endgame of the last match. No amount of passion, desire, or love could stop the play clock from ticking down.

The Reaper sat there, waiting.

It was Clark's move.

He could tip his king to the side and say, "your game." Let it end for once and for all. Molly and the kids would be taken care of now. They didn't need him.

Or he could open his eyes and face another day. Keep playing until he was down to his last pawn.

It was his move.

Clark slowly levered himself out of bed and shuffled towards the bathroom, wincing at the pain in his shoulder.

"Clark," Molly called. "Not yet. Come back to bed. Just a few minutes."

He turned to stare at her—at the soft curve of her hip under the sheet, her alabaster skin, her sleepy smile. He wanted more than anything to walk back to that bed, to burrow under the covers with her and forget that the world existed for just a while.

But he couldn't. Because he knew now that if he stopped, even for a moment, even long enough to kiss her, he'd never find the strength to keep going. To keep fighting the Reaper day after day after day when he knew it was a losing battle.

He turned away. "Sorry. Not today. I'm already late," he mumbled, hating himself for keeping her in the dark and denying her what she wanted most, but knowing he had to. She was his world; he couldn't go on without her or risk losing her.

As he stared into the mirror, he knew she was going to hate him when she finally found out about the money, but that was okay. Because by then he'd be gone.

And he could stand her hating him for eternity as long as she loved him for the rest of his life.

TO BE A HERO

United States, 2030

BRIAN LEANED FORWARD, HIS GAZE RIVETED ON THE LARGE flatscreen television that covered most of the living room wall. He'd dimmed the lights in the room so that nothing distracted from the tense action playing out before him.

On the screen, First Sergeant Balimor ducked behind a concrete barricade somewhere outside Tadmur Syria, his gun clutched close to his chest as enemy gunfire hit the ground in a staccato rhythm, little puffs of dirt floating through the air with each shot.

Brian could almost smell the dust and ozone of the battle. His hands clenched as he imagined himself there next to the First Sergeant, a gun gripped tight in his hands, adrenaline coursing through his veins.

The sergeant and his men were pinned down by at least ten insurgents. He and his soldiers had made a mad dash for safety across a litter-strewn courtyard, one man providing cover fire as the others threaded their way through a maze of broken concrete and rebar.

But now there was nowhere else to go. They were stuck, trapped.

First Sergeant Balimor called in a strike on the enemy position. It was amazing how precise bombing runs had become since the networks took over the war. Even two years ago, the sergeant could've never called down a bomb practically on top of his own head without even flinching. But now he could.

As the insurgents continued to fire at the barricades where First Sergeant Balimor and his men waited for rescue, Tanya Young, Brian's favorite reporter—she looked like an angel with her soulful blue eyes and honey-blonde hair—took shelter next to the sergeant.

"First Sergeant Balimor." She flashed him a dimpled smile as if they were just sitting on her front porch drinking some sweet tea on a hot Sunday afternoon. "Pretty intense fighting back there."

He nodded, his hands still clenched around his gun as another barrage of bullets hit the barricade to their left. Given enough time the insurgents' bullets would cut through the concrete barriers currently sheltering the men. They needed that air strike.

Brian clenched his own hands as he strained to hear the sound of drones approaching.

"Were you scared?" Tanya asked as a grenade exploded about ten feet away. She didn't even flinch, her soft blue eyes focused on the sergeant.

He glared at her for a second, his jaw clenched tight. "Was I scared? You mean when I was running across that courtyard with at least a dozen men firing at me?"

"Yes, exactly. Pretty intense. We even cancelled the commercial break so no one would miss what happened next."

Brian knew they kept the broadcasts on at least a two minute delay, just in case, but it *had* felt really exciting when the commentators broke into the normal weekly war recap to take them live to the scene of the intense gun battle outside Tadmur.

Brian had cranked up the volume and moved even closer to the screen. If his mom saw she'd yell at him for ruining his eyesight, but he didn't care. It was just too good to miss.

Brian hadn't even breathed during the time it took First Sergeant Balimor and his men to cross the courtyard. War, man. You just never knew what was going to happen next.

Not like all those stupid reality t.v. shows his sister liked where you knew exactly what was going to happen. Someone was going to cheat or pick a fight or say something insulting about someone else and everyone was going to get all upset and talk about it for half the show. And then right towards the end when the season was almost over everyone would totally make up and become the best of friends and cry out their differences. And of course there was always someone who was going to get drunk as drunk could be and make a total fool of themselves so they could set themselves up to later star on one of those celebrity rehab shows. (After they did the obligatory "dating" show that basically involved everyone hooking up with everyone.)

But this, man. This was real.

This was live war. Somewhere in Syria right now, First Sergeant Balimor and Tanya Young were cowered behind a small concrete barrier with bullets flying all around them.

"So, First Sergeant Balimor, were you scared?" The look Tanya gave the sergeant would make any man want to confess all his secret hopes and fears.

Balimor gave her a long, considering look and nodded just slightly. "Of course I was, Tanya. Any man would be." He held her gaze as he continued, "But I had a job to do. So I put that aside and got the job done. I'm a soldier. That's what we do."

"Of course it is." Tanya beamed at him as another barrage of bullets pounded the hard-packed desert sand mere feet away from them.

Balimor shielded his eyes from the intense sun and stared off to his right. "Here comes the cavalry."

The image switched away to an aerial view from the small drone.

Oh, wow. There were at least fifty insurgents lined up on the other side of that courtyard. And more arriving all the time.

At the sight of the drone they started to run, scattering towards the walls of the distant city.

Brian's mom walked into the room, drying her hands on a pale green kitchen towel. "Turn that crap off. It's time for dinner."

"But, Mom. They're about to do an air strike. Can't I at least wait until that's over?"

"No." She turned off the television. "Worst thing Congress ever did letting the networks fund the war. Like I need your head filled with that crap. Do you ever see the soldiers that die? Or the ones that can never walk again? No. They just show you the heroes, running through fire, dodging bullets, like some frickin' Jason Statham movie. Well, it's not, you know. Those are real men, Brian, fighting a real war."

He frowned at her. "I know. I've watched the live stream on the net." That one was an unedited feed on a twenty-four hour delay. It didn't show one soldier all the time, but there was always coverage of some soldier doing something and he had seen men shot or in hospital beds. That's how he knew it was real.

His mother shook her head, her lips pressed together in disapproval. "You don't get it, Brian. I never served, but your dad did. And let me tell you, from the little he did say when he felt so inclined to talk about what happened over there, it sure as hell wasn't a rah-rah action movie. War is ugly, Brian."

He glared at her. She was wrong. Not about war being ugly. He knew it was. But she didn't get that it had a purpose. At least those men on that screen were doing something with their lives that really meant something. Not like him and his job at the local fast food joint.

She said all that because she didn't want him to enlist. She'd never recovered from his dad getting gunned down in a nowhere town in Iraq, fighting a war that no one back home really understood.

But she didn't get that his dad had been a hero. He'd died saving others. Three men were alive today because of his father.

"Come on. Food's getting cold."

He followed her into the kitchen, stopping to rest his fingers on the picture of his parents on their wedding day—his dad in his crisp blue uniform, his mother in her pretty white dress.

Brian liked to think that if his father had lived he'd be a lot like First Sergeant Balimor—a grizzled old soldier who'd seen it all and done it all and took each day in stride as if it was just another day at the park.

He sat down across from his mother and started to eat in silence. Whether she wanted him to or not, when he turned eighteen next month he was going to enlist. He was going to do something real with his life.

And maybe, if he was lucky enough, someday it would be him telling Tanya that he was a soldier and that's just what soldiers did as he saved someone's life.

He was four weeks into basic training when the man in a perfectly-tailored gray suit and black sunglasses pulled him aside.

"Brian Lake?"

Brian couldn't see the man's eyes behind the glasses, but he knew who the man was. One of the network execs who'd been watching their training for the last week. The man had paced along the side of the training area, whispering to his assistant, never smiling as he pointed to one soldier or another.

"Yes, sir."

Brian stood at attention. The man wasn't an officer, but Brian knew who had the real power here. Just last week the Major had told Private Mason that he wasn't fit for military service and sent him to pack his bags, but before Mason could even leave the field one of the network men had stepped in. Before the end of the day Private Mason—who looked like a young Paul Newman—was right back to stumbling through the obstacle course, holding everyone else back just the same as he had the day before.

"You ready to see action, Mr. Lake?" The man smiled, flashing perfectly white and perfectly straight teeth in a grin that would do a hyena proud.

"Sir, yes, sir. I can't wait to get out there." He had eight more weeks of basic training and then…

Then he'd finally be somewhere doing something that mattered.

"What position you hoping for, son?"

"Front line, sir. I don't care what as long as I'm there in the thick of things."

"Is that so?" The man quirked one perfectly manicured eyebrow at him.

"Well, sir. My brother's friend who just got out said I should go into some sort of supply or support position. You know, fixing helicopters or arranging new contracts for MREs or something like that. He said to keep my head down and survive until I can get my college money. But I told him that's not why I joined up. I joined to fight for my country, sir."

"Is that right?

"Yes, sir. I want to be right there on the front line kicking ass and taking names, sir."

The man threw his head back and laughed. Brian was sure he really meant the laugh but for some reason in that moment the man reminded him of a robot that had been programmed to replicate human behaviors rather than a man who was genuinely laughing.

"I hear First Sergeant Balimor is your hero," the man said once his programmed laughter ended.

"Yes, sir, he is. I..." Brian blushed. "Well, sir, I like to think that maybe if my own father had survived his time in service that he'd be a bit like the sergeant." He stared at his shoes as his cheeks burned with embarrassment.

The network man clapped him on the shoulder. "Well, son, how'd you like a chance to serve with him?"

"Sir?" Brian tried not to look as excited as he felt. "That would be... that would be a dream come true, sir."

"Good. I'll talk to your commanding officer. We'll have you in the field by next Monday."

Brian stared at him. Next Monday? But...

He licked his lips. "Sir, that would be...I'd love the opportunity, sir. But my shooting. I'm only at thirty percent accuracy, sir."

The man nodded, his lips pressed into a tight little smile. "I know." He glanced around before leaning closer to Brian as if sharing some vital secret. "See, son, we really don't want you to be a hundred percent accurate. I mean, there's such an imbalance already between the technology available to our soldiers and the technology available to the insurgents that it's hardly a fair fight these days. There has to be at least the possibility that we might lose or no one will watch the shows. We need conflict. Tension. Emotion. It can't be too easy."

Brian bit his lip. "But I thought we were there to win, sir. Isn't the point to get in and get out as soon as possible? You know. To protect our interests with the lowest loss of human life."

"Well..." The exec bobbed his head from side to side, nodding yes while really saying no. "You would think that. But, see, son, the problem is this: If we go in there and win in a day or even a week then the American public isn't going to get behind the conflict. And next time we go somewhere they won't watch. They don't watch, the show gets cancelled. And then where are we?"

When Brian wrinkled his brow in confusion, the man pulled him closer. "Don't you see? That's the problem Congress ran into. They'd actually become so efficient at winning their little conflicts, couldn't even call them wars anymore, that no one wanted to fund the troops. They didn't see the need."

The network man paced back and forth, rubbing his hands together in excitement like he was talking about the greatest invention since sliced bread. "See, now, we, the network, we know better than to make that same mistake. It's a balance, son, and a delicate one at that. You want to show our troops struggling to win, show them taking some hits here or there. But you also want to show them winning. They have to defeat the enemy at the end. I mean, they are the heroes after all." He held Brian's eyes with his. "But it has to come at a cost. It has to be fought for. People need enough time to really get behind the troops and believe in them. You see what I'm saying, son?"

Brian didn't, but he nodded as if he did.

"Now don't worry. We try everything we can to bring you

boys back whole. No one wants to see a young man with a missing limb or a missing eye. That's not good for optics, if you know what I mean. That makes people ask awkward questions. And there's some amazing technology these days if you get there in time."

The man stared off into space. "Of course, one or two is okay. It's poignant. Really tugs at the heart strings and lets us know this is something worth fighting for. But hundreds? Well that just shuts the general viewership down, you know? Who wants to watch the weekly broadcast if that's what they're going to see? This isn't *Game of Thrones*, son."

He frowned at Brian's puzzled expression. "Probably before your time. Anyway. So we keep you alive and whole. But beyond that we have to keep people watching, too. There has to be some conflict and risk in there. You get what I'm saying, son?"

Before Brian could actually respond, the man slapped him on the back. "Good. Can't wait to see you on the front lines. With that baby face of yours, they'll eat you up, son. I bet we'll see a two or three point jump in ratings, minimum."

He walked away leaving Brian standing in the middle of the training ground, scared and confused, but excited as hell to finally get a chance to meet his hero and do something real.

As Brian stared out the window of his Humvee, watching the sun-drenched desert dunes undulate beyond the window, he imagined how proud his mother was going to be when she saw him on the weekly newscast. They'd already interviewed him three times about what it was like to head to the front lines.

Was he scared? Was he excited? Did he have a girl back home waiting for him?

(They'd loved it when he said no. The exec had given him a big fake thumbs up sign and a wink.)

Brian wondered if Sarah Fielder would be watching. Maybe she'd look up from her waitressing job at the Hoof N Horn some night and see him on the screen. He could imagine it now:

She'd watch him wipe the sweat from his face as he grinned in triumph after a successful mission, and she'd realize what she'd missed out on. She'd see that Brian wasn't just the runty little kid she'd grown up with but a real man. A hero. And maybe when he came back she'd actually let him take her out for dinner or something.

Hell, maybe she'd buy him dinner.

He grinned to himself, picturing what it would be like to come back a hero, a man who'd done something with his life.

Assuming he even bothered to go back home. Maybe he'd go straight to Hollywood or New York.

Just last week he'd seen Specialist Reynolds, one of his other favorites from the war coverage, doing a deodorant commercial for Mitchum. Rumor was they'd let him out of his enlistment early so he could star in a movie with Maggie Pierce—possibly the most beautiful woman who had ever walked the face of the planet since the dawn of time.

Reynolds had just been a small-town farmer from Idaho before he enlisted and became famous for rescuing a small boy from a burning building during one of the first offensives of the war.

If he could do it, so could Brian.

Brian pressed his face against the glass as the tents of the forward camp came into view. He was about to change the world.

How cool was that?

It was so hot he could've probably cooked a steak on the top of the Humvee if he'd been so inclined. (He wasn't.)

There was a breeze blowing, but it didn't make things any cooler. It was more like having a blast furnace blowing in his face, except worse, because the breeze brought with it fine particles of sand that quickly found their way through every gap in his uniform.

Before he knew it, he had sand down his shirt and in his socks. It clung to his sweaty skin and rubbed against his clothes with every step. Not a lot, but just enough to let him know it was there.

He shifted his shoulders, trying to dislodge the sand between his shoulder blades but failed miserably.

"You Lake?"

It was First Sergeant Balimor. Live and in the flesh.

He was taller than Brian had thought he'd be—probably a good six-four. He had the craggy features and squint-eyed glare of a man who'd spent his life in harsh climates fighting for what was right.

He spat to the side of Brian's shoe and moved a big wad of chewing tobacco around in his lip. Brian had never seen the man chewing tobacco on screen, but he'd heard that lots of soldiers used it to keep awake, preferring it to the stim-packs the network provided.

"Yes, sir, First Sergeant Balimor, sir." He couldn't hide his smile as he straightened to attention.

The sergeant looked him over from head to toe and back again. He didn't crack a smile. "How old are you?"

"Eighteen, sir."

"You sure of that? You look about fifteen."

"Yes, sir."

Balimor spat again. "And how much training did they give you before they shipped you here?"

"Four weeks, sir. I'm up to forty percent accuracy on my shooting." He was very proud of that extra ten percent he'd achieved in the week before they shipped him out.

Balimor glared over Lake's shoulder, his jaw clenched so tight Brian worried he might break a tooth.

"Sir, if I may, sir."

Balimor met Brian's eyes with his steel-grey ones. "What?"

"I just wanted to say what an inspiration you were to me, sir. I watched you every week on the live broadcast. You're a true hero, sir."

Balimor snorted. "Damned networks. Follow me." He turned and walked towards a row of dun-brown tents on the edge of camp.

As Brian hurried to catch up, he saw Tanya Young. She was even more beautiful in person. Brian tripped he was so busy staring at her.

Tanya saw them and made a beeline in their direction. Sergeant Balimor tried to step around her, but she blocked their path. "Brian Lake? Oh, welcome. We're so excited to have you here."

Balimor glared as she gripped Brian's hand and smiled at him.

"Thank you," Brian managed to stutter.

Tanya Young knew who he was and had touched him. The most beautiful woman in the world had touched his hand and said she was excited he was there. That was better than any scenario he'd ever imagined.

"This another one of your damned tricks, Tanya?" Balimor's jaw twitched as he glared at her. "He's a frickin' kid, Tanya.

Hasn't even been trained. Seasoned soldiers not good enough for you anymore?"

Tanya glared back at him. This was a side of the pretty newscaster that Brian had never seen. "We have to keep it fresh, Don. Only so many times 'I'm a soldier, it's what I was trained to do' is going to play with the American people."

She turned back to Brian and flashed him her prettiest, sweetest smile. "You can just see that Brian here is a natural charmer. Aren't you?" She winked at Brian and he almost collapsed right then and there. "Look how all-American he is. He's like every mother's son. The perfect doe-eyed boy next door. They'll really connect with him back home."

The sergeant shook his head. "You're going to take it too far one day, you know that? This isn't frickin' Hollywood. Real men are dying here."

"Not your men." Tanya's smile disappeared for a brief second and Brian caught a glimpse of something darker hidden beneath her pretty smile and soft blue eyes. But then the smile was back and she turned it on him full-force and he forgot the feeling of uneasiness that had gripped him for just that second. "It was nice to meet you, Brian. I'm sure I'll be seeing you again, so you better start thinking about what you're going to say when I come to interview you in the heat of battle."

She winked before turning and sauntering away. Brian couldn't help but watch the way her hips swayed from side to side with each step.

"That woman is a parasite. Stay as far away from her as you can. Now let's go." Balimor headed for the tents again, walking even faster than before.

Brian ran to catch up with him. "Why do you say that, sir? You're always so friendly with her on the broadcasts."

Balimor snorted. "Orders are orders, son. My superiors

tell me to play nice on camera, I do it. But don't for one minute think that woman cares about you or any one of us. If you were dying on the ground, your last breath about to leave your body, Tanya would be right there next to you hoping you lived long enough to give her one last sound bite." He spit on the ground. "You notice she wasn't sweating?"

Brian nodded.

"That's because under her uniform she has a temperature-controlled suit that makes it feel like a balmy seventy degrees out here. All of the reporters have 'em. You think they'd give something like that to us common soldiers?"

Brian shrugged.

"Of course not. Wouldn't be authentic. What would be the interest for everyone at home if we didn't look like we were suffering in the desert sun? Oh no. Have to keep it real. But not too real." He grabbed a rifle from a passing soldier. "You see this?"

"M-16."

"Yeah. Might as well shoot blanks for all the good it does us."

"What are you talking about, sir?"

He unchambered a round. "No real bullets, son. At least not on our side. Someone complained to the network that it was too bloody. There were too many dying at the start of the war. So they took our bullets away. Replaced them with tranquilizer rounds and rubber bullets."

Brian laughed but Balimor stared at him until he stopped.

"You're kidding, right? This is what you do to all the newbies? Haze us a bit with crazy stories about not having bullets and..." He trailed to a stop.

Balimor was staring at him with such sorrow, he realized it wasn't a lie.

Brian swallowed heavily. "Do the insurgents have tranquilizers, too, sir?"

Balimor laughed, a loud belly laugh that shook his whole body. "Of course not. They're actually fighting a real war." He gave the man his rifle back and motioned for Brian to keep walking.

"Aren't we too, sir?"

"No." Balimor stepped close enough that Brian could smell the tobacco on his breath. "If we were fighting to win this war, we'd've been done six months ago. We're here to earn the network money and don't you forget it."

"But..."

"Don't think too much about it, boy. You won't like where your mind goes. Just keep your head down, do your time, and get the hell out of here as soon as you can. And, whatever you do, do not catch the attention of the network types. Trust me." He stared in the direction Tanya had gone, his lips pressed into a tight frown.

***

Brian clutched his rifle tight as he followed along behind Private Morris—a short black guy from Indiana who had two kids and a young wife back home and who liked the Beatles more than anything on this planet. They were in a small little village town somewhere outside Tadmur. Brian really didn't know where, and after ten days on patrol, he really didn't care either.

The sand that had stuck to his skin the first day seemed to be permanently embedded in his flesh at this point and he was amazed he even had any moisture left in his body to sweat. The little village they were in was abandoned, not even a chicken pecking at the dry ground, but they had to clear it.

There'd been word of a gathering group of insurgents some-where in the area and his unit had been assigned to find them.

Find them. Not engage with them. As soon as they found the insurgents they were supposed to radio in the position and fall back to wait and monitor. First Sergeant Balimor's orders.

After ten days of patrol, Brian was starting to wonder how he'd ever considered the man a hero. He was more cautious than Brian's late Grandma Edie who hadn't left her house the last five years of her life out of fear that a rabid cat would attack and kill her. (Ironically, she had died of rabies. But not from a rabid cat. From a squirrel that had wormed its way into her attic somehow.)

Brian hadn't seen hide nor hair of Tanya Young since that first day. When he'd asked about her, Morris had informed Brian he was better off figuring out how to be a soldier than a celebrity.

Brian hated the way they'd all looked at each other when he told them he'd had only four weeks of basic training and shot with forty percent accuracy. One of the senior men in the unit, Specialist Pierce—a man who looked like he'd swallowed at least three people he was so big and broad—had stood up and left the tent after directing an ugly glare in Sergeant Balimor's direction.

They all called him PV-Nothing and never spoke to him.

All Brian wanted was to fit in and do his family and country proud. He didn't understand why they hated him so much. But he'd always been a quick learner, so he spent every free moment he had trying to get better. Already he was up to sixty percent accuracy with his shooting.

The men still seemed to hate him, though. He was paired with Morris because Morris had literally drawn the short straw.

In the distance, they heard the staccato sound of gunfire.

Morris's radio blared a chorus of chaos and bloodshed. "Help, I'm hit." It was Pierce's voice. He and Kinsley were clearing the east side of town.

"Let's go." Morris raced towards the sound of gunfire.

Brian wanted to hang back, maybe think about this for a second. They didn't know how many men there were or what kind of positions they'd taken. Morris could be running right into a trap.

But he didn't want them to think he was a coward either. So he ducked his head, said a prayer to a god he'd never bothered to acknowledge before, and dashed off after Morris.

It didn't take them long to reach the site of the fighting. They were lucky. They'd come in behind some of the enemy shooters.

Morris signaled him to circle right as he circled left. Brian positioned himself behind two men who were entrenched behind a small wall. As he watched, one reached for a grenade.

No time to think; Brian shot the man in the back.

He would've liked to be the type of soldier who could take down the enemy with one clean shot like he'd seen in all those sniper movies, but he wasn't.

It took him a good ten shots to take the two men down.

Morris took down at least five men while Brian was shooting his two.

They both raced forward to check on the insurgents. Because the bullets weren't live ammo, First Sergeant Balimor said they had to hog tie anyone they shot. Helluva lot better than thinking you'd taken down an enemy only to have them wake up and shoot you in the back.

(Funny how that had never been in any of the live war footage Brian had watched back home.)

Brian quickly tied his men up and raced over to Morris's side.

"Here." Morris handed him one of the men's guns. He grabbed another one and checked that it was loaded and ready to fire.

"But..."

Morris looked at him. "How long you think it's going to take before one of us gets shot if we keep playing at war with fake bullets. You think that grenade was fake? Well, it wasn't. That man would've killed Pierce and Kinsley without a second thought. Wake up, boy. If we ever want this war to end, we actually need to defeat the enemy, no matter what the networks want."

Brian checked his gun with trembling hands. "Alright, sir. Where to now?"

Morris aimed the gun at the five men on the ground and shot each one. "We'll circle round, see if that was the last of them."

Brian stared at him, unable to form words.

Morris walked over to the two men Brian had captured and shot them, too, before continuing towards the sound of additional gunfire.

Brian stumbled after him. "Sir. You..."

"I what?"

"You shot those men, sir."

"Only after they tried to shoot our men."

"But, sir. They were..."

"Defenseless?" Morris whipped around to glare at him. He spoke low and fast, spit flying from his mouth. "And what do you think you and I are every damned day walking around in this hellhole with rubber bullets and tranquilizer darts? Get with it, boy. This is war. People die."

As they came around a corner, Tanya ran up to them. Morris cussed under his breath.

"Private Morris, Private Lake. Seems this town wasn't so

deserted after all. You two okay?" Her smile was plastered to her face, but she kept glancing at the guns in their hands.

Morris walked past her as if she didn't exist.

Brian gave her an apologetic smile and followed.

She trotted along at his side. "Private Lake, how's it feel?"

"How's what feel, ma'am?"

"Being shot at for the first time?"

He scanned the rubble ahead, looking for any sign of more insurgents, but there weren't any. "Ma'am, it's not safe here right now. I think you should maybe go back until we've cleared the area."

She laughed. "Oh, I'm just fine, Private Lake, don't you worry about me. But I would really like to know how you're feeling right now." She stared into his eyes with her pretty blue ones and he suddenly thought how nice it would've been to take a girl like her to prom. "Brian, America wants to know how you're feeling. Your Mom's out there somewhere. Anything you want to say to her?"

He stopped and stared at her. His mom? He was in the middle of a half-destroyed city, men could start shooting at him any moment, he'd just watched his fellow soldier kill seven men in cold blood, and she wanted him to think about his mom?

Morris turned around. "Lake, get it in gear."

Brian shook his head and ran to catch up with Morris, Tanya close on his heels. As they paused to scan an abandoned courtyard, Tanya studied the tablet in her hands.

Morris signaled Brian to follow him to the left and started forward. Brian was about to follow, but he noticed Tanya hanging back, chewing on her lip.

He didn't even have the chance to ask if she was going to be alright before bullets ricocheted off the wall where Morris was.

Brian crawled forward and looked around the corner. Morris was there, hiding behind the inadequate shelter of an abandoned motorcycle. He'd been shot in the leg and was busy tying a tourniquet above the wound.

More shots hit the ground to his right and Brian shot back at the unseen assailants.

"Morris. What can I do?" he shouted.

"Help me get back. I'll cover us."

Brian crawled forward as Morris fired off shots towards the other end of the courtyard. Brian just knew that a bullet was going to crash into his spine at any moment. He could see it crashing through his skull, ending his life before it had even begun.

And his mom, the mom he hadn't wanted to think about in the midst of this place, what would she do when she heard? When she *saw* the coverage? What would she do when they played the final moments of his life over and over again, stopping just short of showing the bullet exiting the back of his skull?

Would she think it was poignant, whatever that meant? He doubted it.

Shots hit the ground mere feet away from Morris, but none came closer. Brian grabbed Morris and dragged him back around the corner.

Tanya was there with her pretty blue eyes and easy smile. "Private Morris, that's one nasty wound you have there."

He glared at her. "You say another f'n word right now, lady, and I swear you'll regret it."

Tanya's smile disappeared for a minute and her eyes, still the blue of a summer's day, turned flat and ugly. "I'm just doing my job."

He laughed. "Yeah? Guess that didn't include warning me I was about to walk into an ambush."

"I'm a reporter. Can't interfere with the story, now can I?"

Brian stared at her. "You knew they were there? How?"

Tanya shrugged and Morris answered for her. "Those little tablets of theirs. Shows the insurgents and the soldiers. But don't ask to see one. That wouldn't be *fair*. Because, you know, war is all about fairness."

He winced as he settled back against the wall and thumbed the radio on. "Pierce. Kingsley. Copy?"

"Pierce here. You almost to us? Not sure how much longer we can hold out here."

Morris shook his head even though the man couldn't see it. "Ran into a little unfriendly fire ourselves. PV-Nothing is fine. I'm hit."

"Luck of the idiots, huh. How bad?"

"Bad enough I can't come your way. You want me to send Lake?"

Brian's stomach lurched.

They couldn't possibly think that was a good idea.

Tanya winked at him, her sunny-day smile back in full effect. "Not even here two weeks and already you get your chance to be a hero. Pretty exciting, isn't it?"

She was right. This was his chance. And here he was shaking like a dog in a thunderstorm.

Pierce's voice crackled from the radio. "No other choice. Yep. Send him."

Morris handed Lake the radio. "You heard him. Go find Pierce and Kingsley and help them get out of here."

Brian stared at the radio like it was a deadly snake. He felt like puking. He didn't want to move through that courtyard. Who knew how many men were there just waiting to gun him down.

"What about you, sir?"

Morris leveraged himself to a standing position. He

winced as he put weight on his injured leg, but managed to stay standing. "I'll make my way back the way we came." He glanced at Tanya with a slight sneer. "I suspect that way's clear."

Tanya met him glare for glare, but she didn't say anything.

Brian glanced towards the courtyard where Morris had been shot. "But how do I get across that courtyard, sir?"

Morris smiled. "You don't. Take the canary here and find a different path."

As Morris started to make his slow way back towards the edge of camp, Brian looked at Tanya. Would she help him?

An action hero would grab her and shake her, demanding to know what she was keeping from him. But he was no action hero. He was just a scared eighteen-year-old boy who wanted to survive to see his mother one more time.

"Tanya, what's the safest way to get to Pierce?"

She stared at him with those blue eyes of hers, innocent as a newborn lamb. "Private Lake, I'm just a reporter. I don't participate. It would be against my journalistic integrity to tell you where the insurgents are. And think how I'd feel if someone was killed because of what I told you."

She looked at the rifle in his hands with a sad little moue of disappointment.

He tightened his grip on the rifle and turned away from her. What Morris had done wasn't right, but he'd be damned if he was going to move forward without a real gun in his hands.

Even if he didn't really know how to fire it all that well.

Well, he knew that the way they'd come was clear. And he knew those men had been carrying grenades.

Brian raced back in the direction he'd come, his shoulder blades itching with every step, but Tanya stayed right with him, his early warning of approaching danger.

He rifled through the men's gear, trying not to look at the

very real, very red blood splattered on the ground or notice the gruesome damage a close-up gunshot wound can do.

Tanya stood to the side, her expression flat as she stared down at the bodies. Brian was about to make some excuse for what Morris had done when Tanya shrugged. "You do what you have to do to win. Not that this'll make it on the evening broadcast, of course. You want your ten minutes of fame, you better do something we can actually show."

She stepped over the body of the right-most man and came to join him.

In that moment, Brian wanted nothing more than to go home. Sure, he'd signed up for the war with the full intention and expectation that he'd have to kill someone one day. But this.

This wasn't at all what he'd thought it would be.

He made his careful way back towards the sounds of inter-mittent gunfire where Pierce and Kingsley were pinned down, Tanya on his heels.

As he turned a corner, she lagged behind him and he immediately stepped back. "What?"

"Nothing. We want some good footage of you the lone hero. I'm just the reporter, remember? I can't be tagging along at your heels like I'm helping you, now can I?"

He ripped the tablet out of her hands. The screen showed one blue dot, four green dots, and too many red dots to count. Most of the red dots were clustered around two green dots, but there were a handful positioned just around the corner from the one blue dot and one green dot that were next to each other.

Brian shoved the tablet back into her hands. "Yeah, I see. All about that journalistic integrity of yours, is it?"

He pulled the pin from one of the grenades and flung it in the direction of the red dots on the screen. Not close enough to hurt them, but close enough to block their access to him and Tanya.

As the grenade exploded, he grabbed the tablet back from her.

"Would you stop that? It's going to be a pain to edit out in post."

He glanced at her and then focused on the screen. "I'm a little more concerned about making it through the day, you know."

She crossed her arms and leaned against the wall. "And I had such high hopes for you. You know I'd already reached out to some of my contacts back in Hollywood? They had the perfect script for you."

He stared at her. "We're in the middle of a war zone. Do you get that? Morris was shot earlier."

Tanya shrugged. "He won't even be limping come tomorrow."

"What do you mean?"

Tanya refused to look at him.

"Tanya?"

She sighed and glared at him. "We have something new. Hasn't even been approved for general use yet. Heals you up like that." She snapped her fingers. "So as long as you don't take a shot to the head or a shot to the heart, you'll be just fine and good as new tomorrow."

Brian wanted to ask more, but just then his radio crackled. "Lake, where the hell are you? We can't hold out much longer."

"On my way."

Brian wove his way between the crumbled buildings until he reached a large courtyard, bigger than the one where Morris had been shot. It looked empty, but he knew better by now.

He grabbed the tablet back from Tanya, ignoring her affronted glare.

On the other side of the courtyard, in a small building, were two blue dots. Between Brian and those dots there were at least fifty maybe more red dots. They'd all clustered together at the far end of the courtyard—away from Pierce and Kingsley, but too close to Brian for him to successfully reach them without risking his life.

He scanned the map on the tablet, but this was the only possible path to get to Pierce and Kingsley.

Brian took a deep breath.

He had no choice. He had to rescue them.

"Take cover," he called into the radio.

Brian pulled the pin from another grenade, whipped around the corner, threw it in the direction of the red dots, and then ducked back.

"What did you just do?" Tanya demanded as a horrific blast shook the ground.

The air filled with the dust of exploded buildings and other less pleasant materials. Tanya stared at him, her mouth slightly open.

"What? It was the only way for me to reach Pierce and Kingsley without getting shot."

"But they hadn't even fired at you. What were you thinking?"

"I was thinking there were fifty or more men between me and Pierce and he was running out of time."

"But…"

"You're the one that said I had to do what I had to do."

She shook her head. "You have no idea what you've just done."

"Yes I do. I've cleared a path so I can rescue my fellow soldiers."

Just like his father had.

He grabbed the tablet from her hand. Where before there had been dozens of little red dots clustered at the far end of the courtyard, now there were just a few. The rest were gone, obliterated from the map. Dead.

A handful were making their slow way away from Pierce and Kingsley. Let them run. All he cared about was rescuing his fellows.

He handed Tanya back the tablet and grinned at her. "You told me it was my chance to make a difference and I have. Now let's go get our men."

He could just picture how proud his mother would be when she saw him on the screen, helping Pierce limp his way back to their Humvee.

Brian kept low as he raced along the wall of the courtyard, eyes scanning for any sign of the enemy. He didn't know where those three final red dots were.

His shoulders tensed, waiting for a man to stand up from the rubble, gun in hand, ready to kill him.

But no one moved.

Brian slowed as he reached the area where the grenade had exploded. The dust from the explosion still filled the air and he coughed slightly as it clawed at his throat.

As he stepped forward, Brian saw a small hand peeking through the rubble, the little fingers moving feebly.

So small.

Too small for a man, surely.

Oh no. A woman?

Worse. A child.

Brian sobbed as he clawed at the concrete covering the small figure, throwing bits and pieces to either side.

"Lake? You copy?" Pierce called on the radio.

Brian ignored him as he continued to frantically dig

through the rubble. His fingers bled where he'd cut them on the jagged chunks of concrete, but he kept going, desperate, begging, praying that the child was still alive.

And secretly hoping he was wrong. That it was a man. A man with a rifle and five grenades.

Tears poured down his cheeks. He didn't even realize he was muttering over and over again, "Please be alive, please be alive. Hang in there. I'm going to save you," as he dug and clawed at the concrete and metal that buried the little body.

Finally, he managed to clear the wrecked remains of the building from the tiny figure buried beneath.

A little boy. Maybe six or seven-years-old.

The child opened his soft brown eyes and looked into Brian's with fear. He tried to move, to run away, but he couldn't.

He spoke.

Brian didn't know what he said, but the fear and pain in the child's voice was universal.

Brian scooped the child up in his arms and cradled his tiny body to his chest. "I'm sorry. I'm so sorry." He rocked back and forth, holding the child to him as the child's blood poured forth from a deep wound in his side.

Tanya was right there, her eyes limpid and blue and oh so understanding.

"Tanya, where's that stuff you were talking about? We have to help him. Help me heal him."

She shook her head. "How do you feel, Brian? Holding that young boy in your arms. A tragic victim of war."

"Help him," he screamed at her

"No. I can't. I'm just an observer, Brian."

"Help him!" Brian clutched the boy to his chest as the boy's final breath left his tiny little body.

Tanya watched as Brian rocked back and forth with the

boy's body cradled to his chest. Finally, she rested a hand on his shoulder as if to comfort him.

He shook her away. "Why didn't you help me save him?"

She took her hand away.

"Why, Tanya? You could've saved him."

She bit her lip. "It…Those weren't my orders."

"What?"

She shrugged. "The network, they…" At least she had the decency not to meet his eyes as she said, "They thought it would make better footage if the boy died. The medicine we use is expensive and…"

Brian staggered away from her and the dead little boy. He leaned against a nearby wall, gasping for breath.

What the hell was wrong with these people? That they'd let a boy die like that. And for what? Ratings?

———

Brian sat in the common area the next day staring at a spot on the floor like he had been all day. He couldn't shake the memory of that boy's eyes meeting his and how he'd tried to run, to flee the horrible man who'd thrown the grenade that killed him.

Brian had wanted to be a hero and instead he'd killed who knew how many innocent women and children. Because that's what all those little red dots had represented. Women and children.

After he'd recovered himself he'd started to dig through the wreckage. Every body he found. Every single one. Was a child. Or a woman.

All those little red dots. Too many to count. Each one a woman or child.

He'd only stopped digging when Pierce had dragged him

away. By then Tanya had disappeared once more, of course. No story for the American public there.

Pierce had held him back as the drones arrived, dropping their bombs on the little town, obliterating all sign that anyone had ever been there let alone that all those innocents had died.

And it was all Brian's fault. Because he'd gone back and grabbed real weapons. He'd thrown that grenade where he knew those little red dots were.

It was all his fault.

First Sergeant Balimor sat down next to him. "You need to forget about it, son."

Brian stared at him, too shocked to speak.

Balimor leaned forward. "Look. You don't know who was shooting at Pierce and Kingsley. For all you know, those kids all had guns. And the women, too."

Brian shook his head. "No. They didn't."

"I've seen it, son. This is their home. You don't think every single person who can will defend it from us?"

"What are we doing here then, sir? Where are the terrorists we came to find? Where are the men who want to kill us because we're Americans?"

Balimor started to laugh but then stopped himself. He pursed his lips together. "Not sure they ever existed, son. You've seen these people. You've seen how they live. You think they care about us? Or you think they care about feeding their kids and keeping a roof over their heads?"

"Then why are we here, sir?"

Balimor spit a gob of tobacco on the ground. "Because war sells. And if we want to be ready when we really are needed then we need to give the networks a good show so they'll keep funding us."

"That can't be true, sir."

"Seems as good as any explanation I've managed to come up with the last two years."

They settled into brooding silence as Brian thought about what Balimor had said.

That night, Brian watched the war coverage for the first time since he'd arrived in Syria.

On the screen, Tanya smiled back at him with those perfectly white, perfectly straight teeth, and those beautiful blue eyes and golden hair.

Brian wanted to scream. How could she be smiling today when she'd seen what she had yesterday?

"Ladies and gentlemen," she said in her soft, welcoming voice. "War is an ugly business. We all know this. But it's a necessity, too. Our sons and fathers, daughters and mothers, risk their lives to protect our country every single day. Sometimes they don't make it back alive. Sometimes they come back permanently changed. But they do it for us and we respect them for the risk they take on our behalf. Tonight, ladies and gentlemen, you will see the worst and the best of war."

Her sadly sympathetic face was replaced with Brian's tear-streaked face, ten times larger than it was in real life.

"This is Brian Lake. He may not look it, but Brian is a hero. The best sort of man this army has to offer."

Brian flinched away from her words as they played a compilation of images of him from the first day of boot camp when he was practically bouncing on his feet in excitement to his awe-struck expression when he landed in Syria to him standing tall next to the ruins of the building he'd destroyed with that grenade, holding back his tears.

Brian stared at the screen. What the hell?

"We didn't show you this live yesterday because it was just too dangerous a situation, but we can show it to you now."

The screen filled with images of Morris, Brian, Pierce, and Kingsley making their way through the city. It broke away to show images of men with guns slinking up on them with murder in their eyes. The insurgents were just this side of cartoonish in their clear hatred and bad intent.

"Last night, these four young soldiers were ambushed. We can't tell you where, the situation is too volatile still, but we can show you what happened."

Brian continued to watch as the mangled, contorted version of the night before played out on the screen. They showed Morris get shot and Pierce, too. They showed Kingsley trapped in a small room, frantically trying to scan in all directions as the sound of men approaching reached him from outside.

They showed the insurgents, so fanatical and rabid that their eyes almost glowed red as they crept closer and closer to Kingsley.

And then they showed Brian running towards the action, a determined expression on his face, a rifle clutched to his chest.

They showed Brian take down a soldier who was about to shoot Pierce. And another who was about to shoot Morris in the back.

Step by determined step, shot by shot, they showed him eliminate each and every one of the evil insurgents as they stepped forward to kill his friends and comrades.

Brian wanted to puke. He clutched his hands against his gut and stared at the screen, his lips twitching in disgust.

"When the insurgents saw that they were losing, they did the worst thing possible."

The screen flashed to the tear-streaked face of Tanya Young.

Brian stared at the image, eyes narrowed, as he realized Tanya hadn't cried the day before. Not once.

"It was so horrible, Doug. Brian was about to defeat them and they..." She shook her head and turned away from the camera.

It panned over to Doug who stared into the camera with the earnest sorrow of a Midwestern farmer. "What Tanya can't tell you is that the insurgents, in a last ditch attempt to kill Brian and the rest of the men in his unit, threw a grenade into a nearby building."

The screen flashed to an image of Brian staggering under the force of the explosion and Kingsley flinching as the ceiling above him showered powdered concrete on his head.

The Brian on the screen raced forward and started digging at the ruins to unearth the body of the young boy.

"This, ladies and gentlemen. This is what our women and men overseas fight every day. An enemy so callous, so ruthless, so desperate to win, that they would kill their own children."

Those words hung in the air as the screen continued to show images of Brian digging through the rubble and then holding the little boy's body in his arms, begging Tanya to save the boy.

"This, ladies and gentlemen, is Brian Lake. A true hero. A young soldier barely a man himself. Willing to save this young boy's life at the risk of his own."

They showed an insurgent aiming a rifle and made it look like the man was aiming at Brian as he held the boy's body in his arms. A shot was fired and the screen flashed back to Brian, crying in anguish, the boy now dead in his arms.

Brian turned off the television. He shook his head, swallowing down the bile in the back of his throat.

What they'd done...

How could they?

He turned around and there was Tanya, watching him, her charming little smile long gone.

"What did you do?" he screamed at her.

She crossed her arms. "I fixed your mess. You may not believe it, but dead children don't sell wars. At least not when the child is killed by a grenade thrown by an American soldier."

He shook his head again. "This isn't right. You can't do this."

"Too late. Congratulations. You're America's new hero. You'll get to tour schools, kiss babies, cut ribbons. Maybe we can even swing a sitcom appearance or two. People will adore you, Brian. Boys will want to be you, women will want to be with you. That's what you always wanted, isn't it?"

He backed away from her. "But I...I killed that little boy."

She snarled at him, the pretty mask completely gone, and the ugly do-anything truth finally revealed. "Never speak those words again." She stepped forward, spit hitting his face as she continued. "Do you think that's the only story we could tell with that footage? What about the story of the young soldier with battle fever who slaughtered twenty innocent women and children? Would you prefer that? Because we can make that happen, too."

She stepped back, all Southern grace and charm once more. "Your choice, Brian Lake. Do you want to be a hero? Or a pariah?"

He stared at her.

"Tick-tock, Brian. Five minutes until this airs in the States. You on board or not?"

He shook his head. How had this happened?

He wanted his mother. She'd know what to do.

But it was too late.

"Hero or pariah, Brian?"

He thought of his mother, scared but proud. And his father, a true hero.

He thought of everyone he knew and loved and what it would do to them to learn the truth.

"Hero." He stared at his feet, feeling the weight of shame settle on his shoulders.

"I thought so."

Six months later, Brian sat in the corner booth of a small-town restaurant and watched the "live" war coverage playing on the t.v.

He wondered if any of it had been real. If he'd ever seen a real moment from the war or if every single second of coverage had been staged, cut, edited into the story the networks wanted to tell.

He'd never had the chance to ask Balimor. They'd whisked Brian back to the States the next day and he'd spent the last six months touring the country shaking hands and kissing babies.

So many people had told him how proud they were of him, so many boys had stared at him with adoration in their eyes, so many women had smiled at him like he was the only man they'd ever wanted.

And the whole time he'd known the truth.

He was a killer and a liar.

He hadn't meant it, but that didn't change things.

And every day he paid for his error. With every look, with every handshake, he paid.

A young woman approached him, a little boy hiding behind her legs. She was pretty in a small-town way. "Private Lake, is it really you?" she asked.

Brian nodded, not even bothering to smile.

"I'm sorry to bother you, but he just...he thinks the world of you. You're his favorite soldier, you know."

Brian held back the urge to scream as she shoved the little toe-headed boy forward. The kid was probably five or six and he stared at Brian with green eyes full of awe.

"What can I do for you, son?" Brian forced a smile.

"Can I get your autograph?" The kid held out a picture of Lake staring off into the distance, his jaw clenched in determination.

Funny how no one ever asked him to sign a picture of him holding that young boy's lifeless body.

"Sure." Brian signed the photo and handed it back to the boy.

"Thank you." The boy clutched the photo to his chest. Through lowered lashes, he blurted, "I want to be just like you some day, Private Lake." He blushed and hid behind his mother's legs once more.

Brian swallowed the scream that threatened to escape his lips.

"Good for you, son. We'll need men like you to keep America safe." He pushed his way past them, shoulders tight, lips forced into more of a grimace than a smile as he left the restaurant.

This. This was his penance.

To be a hero.

DEATH ANSWERED MY CALL

I answer the phone and hear Dave say, "Christy, I hate to be the one to tell you this, but Joe had an accident."

No. Oh please no.

I'm not sure whether I actually manage to say the words out loud or whether they just echo in my head. In my heart.

I've always known this could happen —Joe's a skydiver and there's always that chance that something will go wrong. He's certainly lost enough friends over the years. But I never believed it could happen to him.

"Christy?"

"I'm here."

"He's in pretty bad shape. The paramedics are with him now. They've got him stabilized."

I stare at the wall, at the photos of us together throughout the years. Hawaii, England, New Zealand…

"Should I go to the drop zone? Or…"

"No. Meet us at the hospital."

"Okay."

After I hang up the phone, I stare around the living room, unsure what to do.

I need to leave. I need to be there when he arrives—to see him before they wheel him off to surgery.

But there are things I should do first. What are they?

I look at the dog. When did I feed her last? When will I be back? Should I call Suze and ask her to come by?

No, not Suze. She'll be too distraught to help.

I overflow the dog's bowl with food. She'll probably eat it all before I even leave the house, but at least I tried.

My computer is still on. A half-finished report stares at me from the screen. Should I call my boss? Let him know what's happened?

No. I can't talk to him right now. I'll start crying and men hate when women cry. Especially bosses. At least mine always have.

I shoot him a quick e-mail, "Joe in the hospital. Leaving now to meet ambulance. Will check in later."

My hands shake as I type, but I force myself to finish.

I slam the laptop shut, grab my purse, and rummage around for my keys.

Where the hell are they?

I can feel the tears coming as I frantically search all the usual spots—the kitchen table, the breakfast bar, the bowl on the living room table.

WHERE THE HELL ARE MY KEYS?

Then I remember.

Damn Joe. He would finally remember to install that stupid key holder the day before he got in some frickin' skydiving accident.

I grab the keys off the conveniently-located key holder and race out the front door, slamming it behind me.

I pull up to the hospital just as the ambulance is arriving. I know it has to be his. Taupo is a pretty small town. Not likely there would be two accidents needing an ambulance at the same time.

Thankfully, George is one of the EMTs. I'm not used to seeing him in his uniform. Usually he's sprawled on our patio watching the sun set after a long day of jumping.

"George, how is he?" I ask.

"Christy." George gives me a quick hug. "It's bad. We did what we could, but… If he makes it through, it's going to be a tough road."

George's partner rattles off a whole litany of information to the nurses who meet them at the door. I hear words like "arrested" and "fractured pelvis" and "punctured bowel," but they don't mean anything to me.

They start to wheel him away, picking up speed.

"Wait! Let me see him. Please."

I can see that the nurses want to keep going, but George stops them.

"Baby? Baby, can you hear me?" I ask, coming up beside Joe.

He can't.

His eyes are glazed—open but not aware. His nose is bloody and there's a huge gash above one eye.

He's wearing one of those neck braces you always see in TV shows.

I reach for his hand, but it's wrapped in layers of gauze, blood already showing against the pure white fabric.

They've thrown a blanket over the lower part of his body, but the lumps underneath aren't parallel like normal feet and legs should be.

The nurses start to move again, taking Joe away from me.

"No!"

George steps between me and the gurney. "Let them take him, Christy."

"No." I fight my way out of his grasp.

Dave grabs me from behind, wrapping me in a giant bear hug. He must've just arrived. "Christy. Come on, girl. Let 'em go."

He cradles me against his chest as they take Joe away.

I collapse, letting the tears finally catch up to me now that it's just a waiting game.

"Come on. Let's get you inside." Dave leads me through the automatic doors and into the pastel waiting room—all muted peaches and teals. Chairs are artfully arranged in discrete units so people can be together and yet alone in their moments of crisis.

I hate it already.

Six hours later, I hate it even more.

The waiting room is crowded with Joe's friends. They sit around and tell funny stories about him or talk in furious tones about what went wrong. Was it the magnetic stows? The packing job?

I don't care. I don't want to hear it anymore.

He's been in surgery for six hours. I just want to know that he's okay.

Each time the swinging doors open, I hope it's his doctors coming to tell us the surgery is over and he'll be fine now.

But it never is.

I'm glad this is a small town and I know people. Not like when my dad was ill and I sat there in that giant waiting room, all alone, too scared to read my book, watching hour after hour of mindless television.

The doctor finally comes out. Dave holds my hand as we listen. The words flow past me—words like "transfusion" and "trying to control the bleeding" and "may never walk again."

I squeeze Dave's hand so hard I'm surprised I don't break something. But Dave just sits there, solid as ever.

I look around. Most of Joe's crew are there, which surprises me. Skydivers are a tough lot. I've been at a boogie where someone died at ten and the next load was up in the air before the ambulance had even arrived.

But this is Joe. He's family.

I feel claustrophobic with everyone huddled around me. All those sad expressions and sympathetic glances crawl along my skin like ants.

I move to a far corner of the room to call my mom and get away from everyone.

I don't want to call her. She's never liked that I'm with Joe. It doesn't matter how many times he's jumped out of a plane without injury (he stopped counting somewhere around 15,000 jumps), she thinks he must be suicidal or stupid or both to do what he does for a living.

Never mind that my sister's husband was almost killed just driving to work. My sister didn't *choose* to be with a "shiftless loser". I did.

I thank a non-existent god when I get her voicemail. "Mom. It's Christy. Joe had an accident at work. He's in the hospital. I'll let you know more when I do."

As I hang up, an old woman stumbles through the swinging doors. I saw her earlier, sitting in this corner, her hands cradling a red leather pouch. She spent an hour begging every nurse and doctor she could to let her see her husband before one finally relented and took her back.

The old woman collapses onto the chair next to me and I reach out to comfort her, driven by some instinct as old as life.

She leans into my embrace and cries, shaking with sobs, mumbling about how she could have saved him if they'd just let her see him sooner.

Finally, the tears stop and she pulls away.

"Thank you," she says in an Irish brogue.

"You're welcome," I reply, once more reserved and awkward with this stranger. "So, your husband…"

I can't finish the question, but she nods. "Passed away. Kidney failure."

"I'm sorry."

I hope no one has to say the same to me. At least not for many years.

"It's alright, girlie. I've been fighting his death for close to ten years now. Something was bound to get through eventually. Last month it was heart failure. The month before, his liver tried to quit on him."

I must give her a funny look because she chuckles and pats my hand. "I know what you're thinking, girlie. Batty old woman thinks she has some control over death when it's all just fate and chance." She pulls out the red leather bag. "But it ain't. Death listens if you talk to her just the right way. I begged her and cajoled her these past ten years. And each time Edmund was sick, each time they had him down for the count, I brought him back."

"I wish I could do that." I stare at the swinging doors, picturing Joe somewhere back there with nurses and surgeons clustered around his body, trying desperately to save him.

The old woman doesn't respond. She stares off into space, running her fingers over the bag in a practiced gesture.

It matches her—all cracks and crevices.

"Give me yer hand, girlie," she finally says after a long silence.

I place my hand in hers, noting the contrast between my

smooth white skin, still untouched by the ravages of age, and hers, spotted and cracked, almost overcome by time. She puts the red leather bag into my palm and then curls my fingers around it, encompassing my hand in her two.

"I want you to repeat after me," she says, in a tone of voice and with a look that brook no argument. "I beseech you. I call to you in my hour of need. Please. I ask that you save this man I love. I ask that you sustain his life. I ask that you bring him back to me."

I repeat the words, fumbling through over and over again until I finally get them right.

The old woman nods, satisfied, and lets go of my hand. "It doesn't have to be exact like, but you need to ask for help at least three times and say please and what you need at least three times. You ken?"

I nod, looking down at the red leather bag cradled in my hand. I don't want to offend her. She just lost her husband. But what am I going to do with the thing? "I...I'm sorry, but..."

Her bony fingers clutch my closed fist, her fingernails digging into my skin. "You make them let you see that man of yours. And then you hold this satchel in your hand and you take his hand in yours and you say the words I told you to say. You do that and he'll live. Death will pass him by for another day."

I want to laugh. If only life were so simple.

"Thank you," I say instead, swallowing all my questions and doubts.

I beg and plead to see Joe, but when they finally do let me see him I almost wish they hadn't.

He's surrounded by machines, long tubes snaking into his body and down his throat.

They say that there's hope, that he almost died, but they managed to pull him through. Six hours of surgery just to get him to the point where he *might* have a chance of living.

They straightened his legs out some, but it still doesn't look right. Trembling, I raise the blanket to see the misshapen, contorted mess that used to be his right foot.

I squeeze his hand, but he doesn't squeeze back. They've given him drugs to keep him away from the pain and the realization of what's happened.

I know he needs it, but I wish he were here. I need him to tell me it'll be okay.

He's the only reason I survived losing my father. How can I survive this without him?

The machine that's breathing for him makes a steady, wooshing sound with each breath. The machines monitoring his pulse and heart rate beep and whir. Otherwise, it's silent. We're alone.

My fingers stroke the red leather pouch. I feel the dry, cracked leather and remember the old woman's certainty as her clawed fingers clutched my hand.

She was so certain. And I'm so lost.

I grasp the little bag with one hand, and Joe's arm with the other. I say the words, "I beseech you. I call to you in my hour of need. Please. I ask that you save this man I love. I ask that you sustain his life. I ask that you bring him back to me."

I cry as I say the words.

I love him so much.

I can't lose him.

And I don't. Through some miracle—whether it was the red leather bag or modern medicine or sheer stubborn will—Joe pulls through.

They move him to a larger hospital and I live in a small trailer nearby, my life reduced to a never-ending cycle of bedside vigils and exhausted sleep.

Joe becomes my entire existence. Everything else fades away.

He's so broken I wonder how they'll ever put him back together.

They show me a picture of his spine. It's a Picasso version of the original—everything warped and distorted.

Eight hours they spend trying to fix it.

It's just one surgery of many.

Thankfully, he's sedated through most of the first few weeks, so he doesn't know what's happening.

Each time he comes out of surgery, I hold his hand and whisper how much I love him, trying to hide my tears. Each time, I grasp the little red bag and ask Death to spare him.

And each time he survives.

I'm so relieved. I can face anything with him by my side, but I don't know if I'm strong enough to carry on without him.

When he finally awakes for good, when they finally take away the breathing tube and pull back the veil that's been shielding him from the truth, he cries.

This man I've known and loved, who didn't even cry when his brother died, weeps.

Each tortured gasp pulls on the incision along his abdomen and moves the metal frames that hold his legs together, but he can't stop.

I want to hold him, but it's impossible with all the tubes and machines. All I can do is stroke the back of his hand and tell him we'll get through this.

It has to get better from here.

It has to.

But it doesn't.

They take his feet—saw through the bones and tissue and leave him with two stumps of flesh just below the knees.

He tries to bury the hurt and pain under stupid jokes, thinking I won't see how scared he is. But I know him too well.

"It's okay, Christy." He squeezes my hand. "This is a good thing. The first step in our new future."

It's a joke, I know it is, but even he doesn't laugh.

I catch him staring at the empty end of the bed and I know he's wondering whether he'll ever be able to return to the man he was before—a man who did whatever he wanted, whenever he wanted.

A man who was free.

We're sitting in his room one night, both pretending to watch the television, when he screams in pain.

"What is it?" I ask, pushing the button for the nurse.

"My foot. It feels like my right foot is on fire."

The nurse arrives, but she's useless. How do you treat pain in a limb that no longer exists?

I hold his hand as he struggles to breathe, but he wrenches it away. "You should've let me die," he says, glaring at me.

"It'll get better. You'll see." I try to take his hand back, but he won't let me.

I settle for grabbing his blanket. "Remember how much my dad hated his first round of treatments and wanted to quit? But look what happened with him. He pushed through and had five great years before the cancer came back."

"Well, now I know why he killed himself when it did," he says before turning away from me.

How could he? How could he bring that up now?

He knows how much that hurt me. He knows.

It must be the pain talking. We just have to get through this bad bit and it'll all be better.

And it will be better. This isn't cancer that sits inside you and spreads its deadly tentacles throughout your body until you finally die. It's just an injury. He'll heal.

Eventually.

He still has his whole life ahead of him.

We still have our whole life ahead of us.

I watch Joe try to master the pain, but it's too much for him.

He hits the button for morphine over and over again like some sort of nervous tic, wanting to get the next dose as soon as it's available.

He tells his stupid jokes about being a bionic man and I pretend to laugh at them, but he can't hide the agony that dances in the corner of his eyes and I can't get rid of the tightness in my chest telling me it isn't going to be okay.

Each day, after he's dozed off, I pull out the red bag, hold his hand, and say my little mantra.

And each day he lives.

In pain. Mangled. Forever changed.

But he lives.

And as long as he lives, we have a chance. We have hope.

One more day and maybe the pain will start to lessen. One more day and maybe he'll start to adjust to his new reality. One more day…

It has to get better. It has to.

He's bitter and unhappy and hates me and everyone else for saving him, but I never consider leaving.

He can't see the way out, but I know it's there. I have to stay with him, to be the light to guide him through to the other side.

One day, as he's thrashing in his sleep, his eyes squeezed tight in pain, I try to change the litany.

I rest my hand on his and I say, "I beseech you. I call to you in my hour of need. Please. I ask that you take away the pain from this man I love. I ask that you end his suffering. I ask that you restore him to who he once was."

His body arches and he screams. The line on the monitor, the one that shows his heartbeat, goes flat.

As the nurses rush into the room, shoving me out of the way, I grab his leg and desperately repeat the correct words. "I beseech you. I call to you in my hour of need. Please. I ask that you save this man I love. I ask that you sustain his life. I ask that you bring him back to me."

They manage to bring him back.

But the pain is still there.

Eventually, he comes home.

They've done all they can—stabilized what can be stabilized, removed what can be removed. Stitched him up and doped him up. But they can't put him back together again, can they?

No.

He takes hours to do the most basic things—turn over, sit up.

Those are the good days.

On the bad days…

On the bad days, phantom pains shoot through his body like red-hot pokers and he screams until his voice fails. And then he screams in silence, the tendons in the side of his neck standing out in stark relief.

There's nothing I can do. No comforting him.

We try everything. He takes morphine and oxy and everything else they prescribe, but nothing works.

Dave brings him marijuana, but it only dulls the edges.

I continue to hope this will pass, that we'll find a way through. I try to stay positive, to stay happy, to see how far we've come instead of how far we still have to go.

But it's hard.

So hard.

And each day, in the brief moments when he sleeps, exhausted to the point where even the pain can't hold him conscious, I take the red leather bag, squeeze it in my hand, and beg Death to stay away.

She does.

We're in bed one night. It's four in the morning and he's screamed himself hoarse. I'm pretending to sleep, but I'm lying there beside him, my face wet with tears.

He turns to me and cups my cheek in his hand in that way that always made me feel like a small child, safe and protected, and says, "I can't do this anymore, Christy." His voice is so weak I can barely hear him.

"What do you mean?" I ask, not understanding what he's trying to tell me.

"I can't do this anymore," he says, louder, wincing at the pain of forcing the words out. "This isn't a life."

"It'll get better. I know it will." I stroke my fingers through his hair. "Just a little longer. Trust me. You can make it through this."

He doesn't answer. His gaze moves past me to somewhere I can't follow.

"Please, Joe…After my dad…after he…please don't say this." I try to get him to look at me, but he won't.

He lies back down and closes his eyes, pretending to sleep even though we both know he isn't.

I lie beside him, crying silent tears, wishing there were something more I could do.

After that, I never leave him alone.

I won't fail this time. Not like I did with my father.

I know things will improve. Joe just has to hang in there long enough to see it, too.

Dave and his girlfriend, Kelly, come to the house one morning and tell me they've arranged a spa day for me.

Dave's the only one Joe will see anymore. Joe banned the

others—said they reminded him too much of what he lost and can never get back.

It's just Joe, Dave, and me in this little hell.

"Go," Dave says. "I'll take care of him."

I look to where Joe's sleeping on the couch, the dog curled up in the space where his feet should be, and shake my head. "I can't leave him alone."

"He'll be fine. You need this. Go."

Kelly grabs my arm and starts pulling me towards the door. "Trust me, this is exactly what you need," she says. "Dave'll keep an eye on him."

"But, Dave…" I can't form the words. Can't tell him that Joe wants to die. Not with Kelly here.

"Go, Christy. I'll be here the whole time."

"Just don't leave him alone, okay? Promise me."

"I promise," he says, and they bundle me off to the car.

At the spa, I can't relax. Every time the masseuse moves from one spot to another, I tense back up, my body refusing to let go.

I call a cab and go home.

And when I get there…

When I get home…

Dave is sitting in the front room and tells me that Joe's sleeping in the bedroom. But that's not possible. Joe's pain won't give him more than an hour or two of rest at a time and never at this time of day.

I rush past Dave and see Joe lying on the bed, his chest hardly moving. An empty bottle of Percocet is on the bedside table—a bottle that had been full this morning.

Dave tries to drag me back to the living room, saying

things about how "this is for the best" and how Joe can't keep living in this constant state of pain.

I twist out of his arms and dial emergency services, screaming at them to come quick. Dave tries to take the phone from me, but I manage to avoid him long enough to shout out the address.

I run to the bed and fall to my knees, fumbling for the red leather pouch.

"This isn't what he wants, Christy," Dave says, hulking in the doorway, Joe's body on the bed between us.

"What does he know? The pain's blinding him. It'll get better, Dave. I know it will."

I repeat the litany over and over until the ambulance finally arrives, Dave watching me from the doorway the entire time.

Joe survives.

They rush him to the hospital, force charcoal down his throat, and pump his stomach.

When he wakes up, he cries. Not tears of pain, tears of despair.

Nothing has changed. The pain is still there, his feet are still gone, and he still can't do all those things he took for granted before. "Leave me," he begs. "I can't do this to you. I can't ask you to sacrifice your life for me."

"But I love you..." I take his hands between mine.

"Then let me go."

"No. You can get through this. I know you can. It'll get better. You'll get artificial feet and be able to walk on your own again and they'll do another back surgery and it'll help with the pain...It'll get better."

He takes my chin in his hand and forces me to look him in

the eyes. "You're thirty-two years old. Do you really want to be with a man who may never be able to make love to you again? Do you really want to be with a man in constant agony? Do you want that?"

"I want you."

And I do. I can't explain it to him, but I just want him.

In whatever form he takes.

***

Joe doesn't try to kill himself again, but he withdraws somewhere deep inside. I accept his silence as my punishment for saving him, but I don't regret what I did.

I stare at the pictures on the wall of our life together—our first date at the town fair, our first skydive together, the week we spent in Hawaii for our third anniversary—and I know we have so much left to do. This can't be the end.

He kept me together when I was ready to quit after my dad died, now I have to keep him together through this.

That's what couples do for each other. Isn't it?

I look at the note my father left. I read his words about not wanting to go through that pain again, remember how he begged me to forgive him for not being strong enough, and I cry.

I won't lose Joe. Not like that.

This pain will pass. I know it will.

And until it does, I'll be strong enough for both of us.

***

Things seem to get better. His pain eases a bit and we slowly start to make progress. Joe even smiles a few times.

But then he gets a bowel infection. We spend hours in the

emergency room, sitting on cold plastic chairs surrounded by kids with the sniffles, before they finally see him.

It's one in the morning when the young man who calls himself a doctor examines Joe. There are bags under the man's eyes and he's blinking like a toddler trying to stay up past his bedtime, but it only takes moments for him to realize something is very wrong.

They rush Joe into surgery, barely saving his life. He's in the hospital for a week.

Through it all, I continue to hold the little red bag, continue to plead with Death to spare him.

And he survives. For another day, another week, another month.

I do research and find an experimental back surgery that could help.

In the middle of winter, frost covering the ground, they operate.

And it works!

He has whole days without pain.

We start to believe, to see a future. We can never go back to how things were before, we realize that. But maybe we can find a way to a new life.

"See?" I say. "I knew things would improve. You just had to hang in there long enough."

His eyes crinkle from joy for the first time since the accident and I can't hold back my tears. We're finally on our way.

I knew it. I knew if he hung on long enough he'd make it through.

But then…

I wake up one morning, the sun just starting to shine through the blinds, and see Joe lying beside me, holding a pillow against his mouth, trying to hide his screams from me.

The pain is back.

Worse than before.

Joe starts taking too many of his pain pills. They don't eliminate the pain, but they let his mind go somewhere else. Dull the edges of reality.

He's abandoned me. Left me alone.

I can't handle it.

I can be strong for him, but I can't be strong without him.

I hide the drugs. Dole them out one by one.

Dave finds him more.

I take those away, too, and forbid Dave from seeing him.

I tell myself this is only a little setback. The pain will go away again.

But I'm not sure anymore.

As Joe screams and begs to die, I kneel by his bedside with the little red leather bag cupped in my hand and I say, "I beseech you. I call to you in my hour of need. Please. I ask that you save this man I love. I ask that you sustain his life. I ask that you bring him back to me."

And he lives.

Day after day, he lives.

But the pain remains.

We try everything. Pressure chambers, acupuncture, massage, mirror therapy.

Nothing works.

They help for an hour, a day, sometimes two. But the pain always comes back.

I still want to believe that we'll come through the other side.

"Soon, baby, soon," I tell him. "It can't continue like this forever."

"Get out!" he screams. "It's never going to get better. Never."

I leave him alone. I'm not sure even I believe what I'm saying anymore.

Then the day comes when it's all too much. I'm lying exhausted on the couch, Joe asleep in the bedroom. I hear a loud blast of sound and race to his side.

There's blood everywhere.

I don't know how he did it, but Joe got ahold of his old hunting rifle.

He's alive, though; he wasn't strong enough to aim it properly.

I call emergency services, begging them to hurry.

And while I wait I take his hand in mine, wrapping his fingers around the red leather bag, and I beg Death to spare him yet again. We've come so far, how can we quit now?

He watches me through slitted eyes, his face expressionless.

They bring him back, but not all the way.

His speech is slurred, his movements shaky. Sometimes he can't find the right words and I see his anger and frustration build day by day.

I see his hatred. Of me. For saving him.

I try to use the little red bag when he's awake and he slaps it out of my hand, grunting his disapproval.

I know he wants me to stop, but…

But I can't live without him. I can't just let him quit like this.

———

As the days go by, his skin turns yellow.

We find ourselves in yet another hospital room, yet another sanitized space with machines and curtains on tracks.

The doctor talks to us about liver failure. He says he can't recommend a transplant given the circumstances.

I argue and fight until he admits that if someone were willing to donate direct to Joe that the hospital would do the transplant.

I smile.

Everyone loves Joe. Someone will do it. I know they will.

We'll get through this, too. I just need to keep him alive until then.

After the doctor leaves, I kneel by Joe's bed and take his hand in mine, holding the red leather bag in the other.

Joe reaches out, stronger than he's been in days, and wrests the red leather bag from my hands. "No," he says, even this one word slurred. "No."

He shakes his head as I cry and try to get the bag back from him. He's crushed it in his fist and I can't pry his fingers apart.

"Please, Joe. Don't give up on me. Not yet."

He makes an angry gesture, telling me to look around, forcing me to finally see what our lives have become.

Pain, suffering, loss.

He struggles to get the words out, but finally they come. "Let. Me. Go."

I bury my head against the side of the bed. His hand strokes my hair as I sob into the blanket. "I don't want to lose you," I say. "Live for me. Please. Don't leave me. Don't give up on me."

"Not living," he says.

He's right. This isn't a life. Not anymore.

I look at the little red bag in his hand, considering. He closes his fingers around it, pulling away from me.

"Wait. Let me try something."

He doesn't want to, but he lets me wrap my hands around his. I stare deep into his eyes as I whisper, "I beseech you. I call to you in my hour of need. Please. I ask that you help this man I love. I ask that you take away his pain. I ask that you…"

I hesitate at the end, but finally finish. "I ask that you take away his life."

I see the hint of a smile as Joe redlines.

It's over in minutes.

The doctors say it was an aneurysm, probably an after-effect of the bullet.

I know the truth.

I called Death and she answered my call.

IN SEARCH OF A FRICKIN' HERO

Ernigan trudged along, head bowed, hand resting on his donkey's bridle as much for support as guidance. The fool animal probably knew the way better than he did at this point. He coughed into his sleeve, choking on the dust of the caravan a short distance ahead of him, hating the clear blue sky and the bright shining sun and the green-leafed trees that lined each side of the broad dirt road.

This area of Bidelbottom was the type fools wrote poems about. Perfect and pristine, where everyone loved their neighbor and no one ever did a thing wrong to anyone and by gum by gosh if something went wrong everyone gathered around to pitch in and help out.

The perfect location to find a hero.

He hawked and spat out the dust clogging the back of his throat, glaring at the wagons of the caravan ahead. He was too poor to actually ride with them, but he'd figured out—about ten years into this ridiculous quest—that if he stayed behind them, head low, never making any sort of move the guards might consider a threat, that he could trail along behind and be just as safe as if he were part of the caravan.

Only disadvantage was the damned dust.

The donkey quickened its pace and he shuffled to keep up. When he'd started out those twenty-odd years ago, he'd had a fine, beautiful horse that he rode proudly, staring down at the world from on high. He'd lost it three months in to a band of hooligans outside Trace.

That was the first time he'd turned his sights towards the Bidelbottom region. What a disappointment that trip had been. He'd followed the medallion right to a preacher with six sons and seven daughters who couldn't for the life of him believe that there was a higher calling than to be a pillar of his community.

Words like 'end of the world' and 'last hope' and 'world's greatest evil' didn't move the man a bit. At least the preacher had offered Ernigan a nice bed and a warm meal before politely suggesting he move along.

Ernigan peered ahead, shading his eyes against the bright sunlight. He could just make out the thatched roofs of the next town. If it could even be called a town. Unless it disappeared over a hillside, it looked to only have ten, maybe twenty buildings all told.

He sighed.

Chances were, this wasn't his destination. But he never really knew until he was right upon the chosen one. Only then did the medallion turn ice cold against his skin and start to glow a blue so intense it was downright embarrassing.

He spat again wondering how it was in all these years of crisscrossing this country, being robbed at least once every full moon, he'd never managed to lose the damned thing. You'd think some enterprising thief would be able to make something out of it. But the only one who'd tried had been a potential chosen one.

That fool boy. Living the life of a gutter snipe. Dirty and so skinny it was a wonder he didn't snap in a breeze. Ernigan had thought he'd be easy to convince. Surely anything would've been better than his miserable scrabbling existence. But the boy'd laughed right in his face. Told him he wasn't born yesterday and wasn't about to go running off with some stranger who told a good tale. And, besides, what was Ernigan thinking asking him to sacrifice his life for the likes of the people around him. No way, no siree, and thank you very kindly for that coin purse I just cut off your belt and the belt, too.

The scamp.

One of the horses up ahead let go a load and Ernigan wrinkled his nose at the stench, pushing the donkey around it. The fool beast would walk right through it if he thought it would get him to water and some oats that much sooner, and then Ernigan would be stuck smelling the results for the rest of the day at least.

He debated dropping farther back from the caravan. The Bidelbottom region was downright bucolic, but he'd learned that appearances could be deceiving three years back. Rode into the most beautiful little town. Everyone had been so friendly. The head man had asked him to stay to dinner and they'd talked and laughed late into the night.

Next morning, Ernigan had woken up buck naked in a ditch, the only thing to his name the blasted medallion.

Luckily for him, there'd been a temple just a little way's away. Hadn't been too concerned about what their neighbors were up to, but they'd graciously given him a new set of clothes and a paltry amount of coins. When he'd asked what he was supposed to do when that ran out, the priest had suggested that perhaps he should work harder at finding the chosen one.

Work harder!

Work.

Harder.

If Ernigan hadn't been a man of god he'd've punched the priest right in the jaw.

Almost had anyway.

He'd traipsed across this land for *twenty* years, seeking the promised one. Eighty-two times he'd given his little speech. And eighty-two times he'd been given some reason or other that particular person wasn't the one he was looking for.

Oh, so sorry. I'm about to get married.

Oh, so sorry, but my dear mother needs me to stay and look after her.

Oh, so sorry, I'm not interested.

Not interested. In saving the world.

Who, when given the chance, wouldn't be interested in saving the world?

Eighty-two idiots, so far, and counting.

The worst had been the girl who'd told him he was too smelly for her to go with. Too smelly? He'd been on the road for years trying to find her and she wouldn't listen to him because he was *too smelly*?

Mumbling to himself, his hands clenching and unclenching as he remembered every single hurt and insult he'd suffered through the years, he entered the small little hamlet. Definitely *not* a town.

Barely a hamlet, to be honest. Only reason he gave it that dubious distinction was it seemed to have both a bakery and a smithy.

His mouth watered at the smell of fresh-baked bread and he drifted away from the caravan towards a quaint little store-front where a young girl stood, her long brown hair in two braids, one on each side of her head. She smiled at him with teeth more white than any he'd seen in years and eyes that sparkled a blue to match the skies.

Leaning against the counter at her side was a brawny young man with black hair and green eyes who reminded Ernigan of a young oak tree. From the looks of him, he belonged to the smithy. He, too, had shining white teeth that he displayed in a friendly grin.

Ernigan hated them both on sight.

So damned happy. So damned perfect. So damned smug with their little country love story and their wonderful, delicious smelling bread and green rolling hillsides and crystal clear water and vigorous health and…

He spat to the side and stepped closer.

"What can I get you, sir?" the girl asked in a voice made for singing to birds while dancing in the center of a forest clearing.

The medallion against his chest turned ice cold and started to glow a brilliant blue. Cussing, he kicked the nearest post.

All that got him was a bruised toe and a lost donkey. The old rogue took that opportunity to pull free and make for a nearby water trough.

Hopping on one foot, screaming for the donkey to come back even though he knew it was pointless, Ernigan turned on the pair. Which of 'em was it? The girl so pretty and sweet she would probably try to save the Great Dark Lord from his evil ways? Or the big, brawny boy so unabashedly innocent he'd probably offer the Evil One his last ration of water because it was the right thing to do?

"I'll see to your donkey, sir." The boy ran after the donkey with a quick nod of his head and a smile.

As soon as he did, the medallion stopped its glowing and returned to normal.

So the boy.

Great.

Another disaster. Knowing his luck the boy would actually say yes but then be so guileless and stupid he wouldn't see the Dark One's tricks until it was too late.

Ernigan debated continuing onward without even trying to convince the boy of his destiny. Surely there were other potential champions out there. Hell, he'd already found eighty-two of them.

Eighty-two no-good, ungrateful, self-centered, worthless "heroes" too caught up in their own lives to worry about anyone else.

The way these things worked there were probably at least an even hundred wandering the world.

Somewhere.

But who knew where.

Probably weeks of walking away. And just as likely to be as horrible a choice as this fool who'd now caught the donkey and was scratching its ears like they were the best of friends.

Ernigan glared as the boy tied the donkey to a post in the shade, put a bucket of water within easy reach, and poured some feed into a bucket. Whistling happily, the boy returned.

Well, if nothing else, he'd probably set up a nice camp each night. And bandits might think twice about challenging someone with arms the size of small tree trunks.

Grumbling silently to himself, Ernigan forced a smile. "Thank you, boy. What's your name?"

"Killan, sir."

"Killan. Good name. What do you do, Killan?" He'd learned long ago that you couldn't just jump into the whole chosen one conversation. You had to start off slow, ease them into it with small talk and chit chat.

"I'm an apprentice blacksmith, sir."

"You like it?"

"Oh, yes, sir. It's the best job there is."

That didn't bode well. Contented folks weren't much interested in going through ten types of hell just to probably end up dead in the end. (Not that he'd managed to convince *anyone* yet, even the most destitute and discontented. He'd even had a prisoner in a stockade turn him down once! Like life could get much worse than that.)

He tried to sound casual as he leaned closer and asked, "You ever wanted to have adventures? You know, travel around, see the world?"

The boy laughed. "Oh no, sir. This is the best place in the world. Why would I want to leave it behind?" He flashed the girl a smile. "Plus, nowhere in the world has a girl like my Lily."

Lily smiled back at him, eyes full of love and adoration.

Ernigan wanted to be sick. Not just because their sappy ridiculous love was too much for a man like him to stomach, but because he just knew that he was going to fail yet again.

After eighty-two tries a man started to get a feel for these sorts of things.

But he had to try. He'd made a vow to his god and he wasn't going to quit and go home, especially not after twenty damned years of this.

He figured it was a numbers game. Ask enough heroes, one was bound to say yes, which meant the only way to fail was to quit trying.

Right.

He pointed at one of the loaves of bread on the counter and slid a coin towards Lily, unable to ignore the rumbling of his stomach any longer even with his potential hero standing there before him. She handed the loaf over and meticulously counted out more change than he'd expected to get back.

He took a bite, savoring the soft crunch and slight tang. He could like a town like this…

Of course, three days in he'd want to scream at all the helpful, too nice folk who wouldn't mind their own business.

Sighing, he studied the boy. "You know, Killan, that's really too bad. Honestly, it's a bit of a problem."

"What is, sir?"

"Your complete lack of desire to leave this beautiful place you call home."

"Why's that, sir?"

It was now or never. He leaned closer, holding the boy's eyes with his own. "I'm a priest of the Order of the Phoenix." He held out the medallion, which was glowing so bright it was almost blinding.

Killan leaned closer to look at it. "That's very nice, sir."

"Can I see?" Lily leaned close to look at it, her hair smelling like lilacs and honeycomb. Not the distraction the boy needed in that moment. "Oh, wow. Killan, have you ever seen anything like that before? Why does it glow blue like that?" She turned her pretty eyes on Ernigan, a dimple appearing in her right cheek as she smiled.

Ernigan narrowed his eyes. Too bad she wasn't the chosen one. She seemed a bit more keen on things than good ol' solid-as-a-rock Killan.

"Well, see, that goes right to the heart of the problem. I was sent into the world by my order to find the chosen one."

"The chosen one?" they both asked in unison.

"Mmhm. There's a great evil that was locked away many, many years ago. Hundreds, thousands of years ago. And that evil has been scratching at its cage ever since trying to get back out."

They watched him in wide-eyed fascination like he was some storyteller and they were young kids gathered around the fire at night.

Didn't they get that this was real? That the Dark One was

right there on the other side of the barrier just waiting to break through and wreak havoc on their world?

Then again, looking around he wasn't surprised they didn't see evil as a living thing that could chew you up and spit you out with no care at all. For them a bad day was probably when the sun got stuck behind a cloud for a minute or two.

He put the medallion away and moved closer, lowering his voice so they'd lean in. "My order has done what we can to keep the evil locked away, but it's not enough. It's almost free."

He wanted them to understand the seriousness of what he was telling them, but after eighty-two tries he was so weary of the whole thing that he just couldn't muster enthusiasm for the story the way he once had, so he skipped ahead to the end.

"When that evil busts free and comes back to this world we're going to need someone who can stand against it and lock it away again." He focused on the boy. "That's you, Killan. You're our chosen one. The medallion shows it. That's why it was glowing blue like that."

Lily clapped her hands in delight. "Oh, Killan, that's wonderful. You have to do it." She beamed a smile brighter than the sun at Ernigan. "Of course it's him. He's brilliant at everything he does."

Ernigan wanted to scream at her that this wasn't some new dance step they were talking about, but he forced himself to nod and smile instead.

Whatever it took to close the deal.

"What do you say, Killan? You in?"

The boy scrunched up his face and shook his head. "I don't know. We just got a big order for horseshoes in and I don't think Smith Niall can handle them all himself. Can you wait a tenday?"

Ernigan gritted his teeth. "This is a bit more important than horseshoes, son. We don't get this evil locked back up, there won't be a need for horseshoes anymore."

Killan laughed.

"What's so funny, my boy?" Ernigan fought the urge to throttle him.

"Well, that's not possible is it, sir? That there would ever be a time when horseshoes weren't needed anymore? I mean, there's always a need for horseshoes."

Ernigan bit his lip. Seriously, this was his hero? This country bumpkin? Not for the first time, he wondered if someone up there really hated him.

"We don't get this thing locked back up, son, we'll all be dead."

"Dead?" Killan laughed again.

"Yes. Dead."

Killan licked his lips and looked back and forth between Ernigan and Lily. "Well that's pretty serious. And you say I'm the only one who can defeat it?"

"Yes. You're the only one. I've spent the last twenty years trying to find you."

Admittedly, that only one bit was a lie. But he'd long ago learned that if you told someone they were one of an indeterminate number of potential chosen ones that they tended not to take things quite as seriously as needed.

"How long will this take?" Killan reached for Lily's hand. "Lily and I are getting married in the fall."

"Oh, we'll have you back in time for that. No problem."

Another lie. But just a little one. Well, maybe a medium-sized lie.

Or perhaps a big, heaping lie so gigantic he didn't even want to think about it.

Killan tugged at his ear. "I'd need to ask my parents. And arrange for someone to take my place at work. And..."

Ernigan wasn't the best of salesmen—obviously, given his eighty-two prior failures—but he was good enough to know that when the chosen one wanted to talk it over with someone else he was about to lose them.

All it took was one well-meaning friend to say, "Do you really want to go traipsing off into nowhere with some complete stranger you don't even know just because he has a metal that glowed blue when it was around you? I mean, that could mean all sorts of things. Are you sure it even glowed blue and it wasn't just some fancy trick?"

He grabbed Killan's arm. "We don't have time for that. I told you, I've been looking for you for a very long time. Actually…" He looked around as if scared. "I think the Evil One's minions have been following me. I wouldn't be surprised if they appear at any moment. If you have two horses we could use, I think that would be best."

"Two horses? Oh no. Nothing like that."

Ernigan eyed the two fine black stallions tied up outside the smithy. "Whose are those?"

"Oh, those belong to Sir Rowlins. We just finished reshoeing them. He'll be by to pick them up later today."

"They'll do."

Killan leaned closer. "You can't just take someone's horses, you know."

"You can when the fate of the world depends on it."

Killan crossed his arms across his chest and stepped back. "I think you have the wrong man, sir."

Damn it. He'd pushed too hard.

The boy wasn't going to go.

Not unless he made him.

Biting his lip, he reached into his pocket. All these years, all these potential heroes, and he'd never used the coin. Just like the medallion, it had stuck to him like a bad infection. No matter what he lost, no matter where he went, the damned thing always seemed to find him again. Black and cold as the darkest night; he hated to even touch the thing. Most days he pretended it didn't exist.

But he was tired and getting old and if he didn't find someone to train soon—something that would take a good decade if he was lucky—it was going to be too late by the time the Evil One escaped.

It was time to try something new.

He stepped away from the boy. "I'm sorry. I went too far. It's just…I know what happens if we don't succeed. And I'd do anything to keep that from coming to pass. But you're new to this fight. You don't understand the stakes."

He gripped the coin in his fist, hoping the boy would change his mind before he had to use it.

He didn't want to do this. He didn't know what it did, but he knew it had to be bad.

Twenty years he'd spent wandering the world, barefoot and bereft, slogging his way through city after town after hamlet after two huts placed somewhat close together after man living in what could only generously be referred to as a ditch and he'd never sunk this low.

But it was time.

Time for a hero to be born.

He threw the coin to the ground and tensed, waiting.

And waiting.

And…

Waiting.

Nothing happened.

He stared at the coin.

It just lay there. Doing nothing.

What the…?

He'd been told to use it. Told it would convince his chosen

one to act. That it would start the chain of events that led to the final confrontation between good and evil. But it was just sitting there on the ground like the stupid lump of metal it was.

All these years, all those stupid fools who'd told him no. And he'd always thought, *I still have the coin.* Always known he had that one last trick up his sleeve if words failed.

But now…nothing.

What if…

He clutched a hand to his chest.

What if this had all been some sort of elaborate practical joke? Some cruel twist of humor played on him by the elder priests? He wouldn't put it past a few of them to bring proud young Ernigan down a peg or two by sending him out into the world on some pointless quest.

They'd probably laughed to themselves thinking what a fool he was to believe he was the chosen one chosen to find the chosen one.

Probably laughed for weeks. Or months even.

But years?

They'd played this prank on him for *twenty frickin' years!*

He balled his hands into fists, ready to march all the way back to the mountain keep where he'd been trained and break down the ten-man-high doors to demand an explanation.

How dare they? How dare they do this to him?

He'd *believed.* In them. In good and evil. In the divine fight to protect the world.

In sacrifice.

And truth.

He'd given his life to finding their hero.

And it had all been a joke?

What manner of cruel men were they to send him on this fool's quest?

Of course it all made sense now.

How had he ever let himself think there could be multiple chosen ones? There would only ever be one. A man of noble heart, flawless at everything he tried, sacrificial to a fault, who never once doubted or questioned his ultimate destiny.

How had he ever let himself believe that the chosen one was some street kid who'd steal a good man's purse or a father of thirteen or a small town bumpkin blacksmith or any of the other eighty-two stupid, foolish, idiotic people he'd found?

Ernigan stomped off towards his donkey, cussing and cursing the fate that had led him to figure this out when he was as far away from the main temple as a man could be and riding a thrice-damned donkey who'd rather find the nearest stream than walk faster than a crawl.

Killan called after him. "Sir? Sir, I think you dropped this."

"Keep it," Ernigan snarled, grasping for the donkey's reins as it moved away from him, still munching on the feed Killan had given it. "You stand still you bag of bones."

Ernigan lunged for the reins as a light flashed behind him and Lily screamed.

He whirled in time to see Killan drop the coin, but instead of falling to the ground like it should have, it spun in the air, glowing a brilliant, malevolent red.

As Ernigan watched in fascinated horror, the world cracked open in a line running upward and downward from the medallion.

"Get away from there. Get away from there, now!" he screamed.

Killan and Lily stood frozen, watching as the crack broadened into a rent and some *thing* stepped through. It was straight out of a nightmare. Scaled and clawed and tusked and dark as the darkest night. It looked so much like what an old grandmother would use to scare a child at bedtime that

Ernigan would've laughed if it hadn't turned its red gaze towards Killan.

"Killan. Here." Ernigan threw him the medallion.

As he caught it, a bright white light shot from his hand, driving the creature backward.

Desperate, Ernigan searched through his packs, pulling forth the sword the priest at the last temple had given him— the third such sword he'd carried in his twenty years of travel. A supposedly "magic" sword that had been amazingly easy to replace each time he'd been robbed and left with nothing.

He ran past the stumbling, blinded creature and offered the sword to Killan. "Here, boy. Use this."

Killan drew the sword from its sheath and swung at the creature. In his hands, the dull gray sword sliced through the creature as if it were made of soft butter, cleaving it in two with one blow.

Killan and Ernigan stared at one another for a long moment as the creature bled black blood onto the ground at their feet, smelling like a charnel house in mid-summer.

"What was that?" Killan asked.

"I don't know."

"Here comes another one," Lily screamed, pointing towards the rift.

Killan placed himself at the breach, slicing and cutting as creature after creature appeared.

"Get the horses," Ernigan ordered, pushing Lily in the direction of the smithy. "He can't hold them off forever."

She ran, skirts clutched high, flashing her calves for anyone to see.

She grabbed the horses and led them back, the smith shouting and chasing after her until he saw Killan slicing and slashing, keeping the nightmare creatures at bay as they tried to pour forth from their dark containment.

Ernigan grabbed an empty sack from the donkey's back and filled it with as much of the bread as he could. (Twenty years on the road had taught him the value of a good fresh loaf of bread.)

Quickly, he pulled the saddle bags from the donkey's back and slapped it on the rump. "Get out of here you fool beast. Go before they decide to make a meal of you."

The donkey flicked an ear at him but trotted off, walking faster than it ever had for him as Lily rushed to saddle up the two magnificent horses.

Ernigan shouted at the villagers to flee. Why did people always seem to run towards evil instead of away from it?

The smith tried to help Killan, but was cut down for his troubles. A normal sword did nothing against the Dark One's minions. It literally bounced off their tough flesh.

Killan was tiring quickly, his strokes slowing, his breathing heavy, but he kept going while the others smartened up enough to run. On foot, most of them. Probably wouldn't last through the night, but that wasn't Ernigan's concern. Not now. He had a hero to train.

He and Lily mounted up. "Killan," he shouted. "Time to go."

Killan ignored him, all his attention focused on the foul beasts before him.

Ernigan readied himself to ride towards the boy even though that was the absolute last thing he wanted to do. Heart racing faster than a galloping stallion, fear sweat making his shirt and pants stick to his skin, he took a deep breath to ready himself.

But Lily was ahead of him. She shouted Killan's name and rode straight for the breach, turning her horse at the last moment and reaching down for Killan.

He levered himself up and into the saddle behind her like

he'd been doing it all his life. He even slashed one last night-mare creature in the face before she turned the horse and headed back towards Ernigan.

As they raced away towards the distant horizon, Ernigan couldn't help but smile. He'd finally found his chosen one.

Who knew it would be so easy?

BY YOUR SIDE WHEN THE SUN SETS

"Gray, wake up!" Hands grasped his shoulder and shook him until he swatted them away. He winced as the motion pulled at the scar tissue along his back, the unfortunate remnant of a battle he couldn't quite remember. They all started to blend together after a couple decades spent dragonback, slashing and fighting in the name of God and country.

As the screams, roars, and strong smell of something burning made their way through the layers of exhaustion he snapped completely awake, reaching for his boots and sword.

"What is it? Are we under attack?" He shoved the boots on, grabbed the sword, and ran into the hallway, the cadet who'd awakened him—young and eager like all the cadets who he could never name but who he always smiled at and nodded to when he passed—trailing along behind him.

If they were under attack that was a very bad sign, because it meant that the forces of the Emperor had somehow snuck past their front lines to attack the very core of Calindar where only the too old, the too young, and the wounded were left to defend the capital.

He pushed forward, following the roars and screams as

women and children rushed past him in the opposite direction, faces coated in soot, eyes wide with fear. The smoke of whatever was burning singed the back of his throat and brought tears to his eyes. He wasn't used to being on the ground when dragons were fighting. He didn't like it.

"How did they get past the front line?" he demanded of the cadet who had to be at least six-foot tall but trailed along in his wake like a lost puppy looking for a home.

"We're not under attack, sir. It's…it's Malinorius, sir."

"Mal?" He stopped in his tracks and the cadet ran into the back of him, quickly backing away, his eyes on the sword in Gray's hand.

"Yes, sir. He's…We don't know what's wrong with him."

Gray let out a long string of cusswords as he raced towards the large sand pit where he'd left Mal asleep just a few hours before. Time was he would've been sleeping out there next to Mal, but old bones required comfortable beds and even that didn't seem to help much anymore. He ached in a thousand different places no matter where he slept or what he took for the pain.

He ran into a scene of chaos, illuminated by the light of a full moon and dancing flames. At least a dozen men were passing buckets along a line trying to put out a stable that was on fire. Another half dozen were trying to wrangle the horses that had been led away from the stable.

But he didn't care about them. He cared only for Mal, his dragon, his companion for the last twenty-five years. Mal might have been assigned to him like you'd assign a cavalry soldier his horse, but over too many campaigns and too many miles to count, Mal had been the one constant in his life. His best friend.

And now Mal stood on his hind legs, three stories tall, bellowing his rage to the world, breathing fire towards the men who encircled him with ropes and arrows ready to bring him down. A young cadet, even younger than the one that trailed Gray, raised his bow, arrow nocked, aiming at one of Mal's large golden eyes.

"You shoot my dragon, I will gut you," Gray shouted, his voice loud enough to carry over Mal's roars and the cries of the horses. He adjusted his hold on his sword, meaning every word of it.

The cadet turned to stare at him, wide-eyed in fear, but Gray didn't know whether it was fear of him or fear of Mal. The boy was too young to have ever ridden dragonback. He wouldn't understand the bond that existed between dragon and rider. They didn't speak mind-to-mind like the stories would have people believe, but when you spend every day of your life, year in and year out, with an intelligent creature, it doesn't matter if you can "speak" to one another or not. You know each other. You understand each other.

The cadet with the bow in his hand didn't know that. But the other men gathered around Mal did. Dragonriders like Gray himself, they formed a perimeter around the dragon, none willing to harm him, but none able to calm him either. And all ready to act if Mal tried to escape his corner, no matter how much they wouldn't want to.

"Let me through," Gray shouted. The riders parted to form an easy path across the sands to Mal's side.

Gray made his way through that human corridor, all of his attention focused on Mal who roared his defiance once more. Three-stories tall, his body covered in scales as large as a grown man's hand, his teeth as long as Gray's forearm, the talons on the ends of each toe large enough to skewer a man straight through...he was a beast straight out of a nightmare.

But he was Gray's best friend, so Gray continued forward, closing the distance between them.

Mal spewed fire into the sky, thrashing his tail from side to side. Gray swallowed heavily. He'd been there when Mal reduced a building to cinders in the space between one moment and the next. And he'd been there when Mal grabbed a man from the ground and crushed him in one taloned hand. And when Mal tore out the throat of another dragon with his teeth.

But he kept walking forward.

He trusted Mal at a level he didn't trust anyone else. Men would lie to you. Women would get tired of waiting for you. But a dragon was loyal unto death. You treated it right, it would be there for you.

Always.

Assuming the dragon actually recognized you, that is.

Mal roared so loud the sand bounced beneath his feet. As Gray came closer, the dragon dropped to the ground, head snaking from side to side, eyes shaded with the red of anger.

Ben, the closest Gray had ever come to a human friend, shouted from behind them. "Gray. Come back before he eats you. We'll keep him contained until he calms."

Gray kept his eyes focused on Mal. "He's not going to calm on his own, Ben. You know that."

He took another step closer. And another. And another.

"Mal? Mal, buddy. It's me, Gray. What are you doing, buddy? Something upset you? Something bite you? You want me to see if I can fix it?" He had to shout, but he kept his voice friendly, relaxed.

As relaxed as he could given the circumstances.

Mal tilted his head to the side as Gray talked, but his eyes still burned red.

"You want a cow, buddy?" Gray asked.

Mal tilted his head to the other side. Cow was a word he knew well.

"Or a lamb? Does that sound good? A lamb?"

Mal thrust his large snout forward. Lambs were a special treat usually reserved for after a battle. Oh, there were usually four cows involved as well, but Gray always made sure there was a lamb first.

The cinnamon scent of Mal's breath washed over him. Gray wanted to step back, but he didn't. Mal had lowered his great big wings and the red was starting to fade from his eyes.

Gray didn't take his attention from Mal as he shouted, "Ben, get me a lamb. Now."

Someone ran in the direction of the pens as everyone else stood, waiting to see what would happen next. Would Gray be Mal's last meal? Or would he truly wait for a lamb to be brought?

As they waited, the stable collapsed in on itself, sending a whoosh of burnt embers in their direction, but Gray didn't turn away and Mal didn't shift his focus.

"That's a good boy. We'll have that lamb for you before you know it." Gray used his words to soothe, not yet ready to step any closer.

Mal rubbed his chin against the sand and Gray laughed softly, finally closing that last few feet. "Here, I can scratch that for you if you'll let me." He held his hand out, waiting to see if Mal would remember.

Scratching Mal's chin was how they'd first bonded back when Mal was just a fledgling, all gangly limbs and wings and only about an inch taller than Gray.

Mal slowly lifted his head from the sands and Gray rubbed at the soft skin under his chin, using his whole forearm on the dry patches along his jawline. Mal made a rumbling noise deep in his belly and pressed down on Gray's arm.

"Whoa. Don't forget you could crush me, little one."

The red was gone from Mal's eyes, but he blinked at Gray in confusion, not understanding.

Not remembering.

Gray swallowed the tears that threatened to overwhelm him. Fortunately, he was rescued by the return of the same cadet who'd woken him, a lamb bleating from the boy's arms as he approached.

Mal's head snapped up and he focused in on the lamb and the boy.

"Drop the lamb and get back. Now!"

The boy stuttered to a stop, finally realizing the danger he was in. Most of the cadets had only dealt with a fully-trained dragon. Raised from a fledgling, dragons knew that men weren't a meal. Only those in extreme pain forgot. Or those like Mal.

Those who…

Gray refused to think about it. Not now. Not standing in the sand pits on a full-moon night, surrounded by men who all knew what came next. What had to happen. Because a creature who breathes fire and stands three stories tall and has talons that can spear a man but can't remember that men are his friend is a danger. A danger to all.

The boy threw the lamb through the air towards Mal and then ran. Lucky for him, Mal was more interested in the lamb than the fool who'd run in the presence of an uncontrolled dragon. The lamb's bleat ended abruptly with the snap of Mal's powerful jaws.

Gray was inured to the grisly sight of his dragon eating, so he stood his ground while Mal's jaws snapped down, once, twice, three times before the lamb disappeared for good with a great big gulp.

By then someone had thought to bring a cow from the

pasture. Mal took the cow in his feet, rending it apart before quickly consuming it, too, in just a few bites.

Through it all Gray continued to stand there, watching, waiting to see what would happen next.

Fortunately for him, and Mal, and the rest of the compound, Mal stalked back to the corner of the sand pit, dug himself a spot, and curled up to sleep.

Gray wanted to rush to his side, to dig himself a spot to sleep, his hand resting on a slender leg with Mal's tail wrapped around him, a reminder to both of them that they weren't alone in this world. But he knew he couldn't. Not yet.

When Gray turned around the Commander was standing there, arms crossed, face impassive.

"Commander."

"Officer Leonel."

They stared at one another across five feet of sand, neither one willing to speak again. In the distance Gray could hear other dragons rumbling their distress to their riders, but in Mal's sand pit the air was heavy with silence as the other riders slunk away into the night, no one willing to stay around for what came next.

"We don't know he has it," Gray finally said.

The Commander snorted. "No? You're telling me that a twenty-year veteran suddenly decided to burn my stables down because he had a bad dream? You know the protocol."

Gray swallowed the words he wanted to shout. A man didn't say those sorts of things to his commander without consequences. "This was the first time. Maybe…"

"Maybe what?"

"Maybe it won't happen again. He could have months. Or years."

"You have to do it now, Gray. Next time it may not be two horses who pay the price but two cadets." He uncrossed his arms and ran his hands through his hair. "You know I don't like this any more than you do. But you know what's coming and what has to happen."

Gray turned to stare at Mal. He was snoring peacefully now, the moon shining against his scales as his chest rose and fell.

"I can have another rider do it if you want." The Commander stepped to his side, voice soft. Once, before he'd been a commander, they'd been comrades who rode side-by-side into countless battles. But his dragon had been killed underneath him and he'd stepped away from riding.

Gray knew the offer was made out of kindness, but it filled him with rage. Twenty-five years Mal had served his country. Twenty-five years of taking wound after wound for something he didn't even understand, all because Gray asked him to. And now the commander wanted him to just hand Mal over to someone else? To let someone else end his life like so much discarded garbage?

"No. If it has to be done, I'll do it."

The commander stood there, waiting.

"Tomorrow. Let me..." He swallowed the tears, locking them away where he'd put all the fear and horror every time he flew into battle. "Let me take him to the lake. Give him one last day. Please?"

He wasn't a man who asked for much, but for Mal he'd ask for the world.

The commander nodded. "Tomorrow."

Only after the commander had left did Gray limp over to Mal and curl up at his side. Mal didn't wake, but his tail wrapped around to pull Gray closer, the heat of his body radiating against Gray's back. Normally that would be enough to let Gray relax and finally sleep, but he didn't. How could he, knowing what was coming?

The next morning Gray stumbled through his morning routine, his body aching in a dozen places after a night spent not sleeping on the cold, hard ground, his stomach hollow with the emotions he refused to feel.

He ignored his fellow riders as they joined him at the breakfast table and tried to engage him in small talk about this person or that, about the war, about the weather, about anything other than the fact that he was about to lose Mal.

This was why it was better to die in battle, to die in glory and fire. Because at least if you died in battle it was quick and it was over.

Being the soldier who came back meant living with the wounds and the memories. And eventually losing your dragon. What was happening to Mal was well-known, but never spoken of amongst the riders.

The Forgetting never made it into the great ballads. No one sang about the heartbreak of losing a life's companion to the fog of time.

They never told cadets about it either. No one mentioned to them as they took those first flights, soaring through the air, free in a way a man never could be anywhere else, that eventually it would end in blood and sorrow.

But they all came to understand the truth sooner or later.

If a dragonrider was "lucky" enough—if he lived through enough battles, through years of close calls and injuries—if that happened, then one day his dragon would forget him. It would turn wild. It would throw off the chains of friendship and turn on any human it saw, including its rider.

It could happen after five years or ten or twenty, but it always happened eventually. The Forgetting.

And when it happened, the rider rode away with his dragon and came back alone. No one ever spoke of the dragon again. It was simply gone. Forgotten in its turn.

Gray had never known whether what was done was done away from the compound to spare the dragons or to spare the riders. All he knew was that every man who'd returned from that last flight returned with a haunted look in his eyes.

He stared at the lumpy porridge in his bowl and knew he'd rather cut his arm off than kill his dragon, but what choice did he have? He couldn't control Mal if Mal didn't want to be controlled.

Ben sat down next to him. "You know it has to be done, Gray."

"I know."

"They'll probably make you a commander. Or a trainer. The boys look up to you. You'd be a good trainer."

He nodded, but he didn't want to be a trainer or a commander. He just wanted Mal.

He glanced at Ben. The closest he'd ever come to making a friend. They'd both been assigned fledglings from the same clutch. But a new rider spends twenty hours a day with his dragon. Feeding it, cleaning it, sleeping next to it so it isn't alone. Bonding. That's all a new rider does.

And after that, when they were sent to fight, well… All Gray had ever wanted after a battle was to find Mal, curl up by his side, and forget what he'd seen and done. Other riders might gather together for a drink and tell one another stories, shaping the chaos of battle into legend, but not Gray.

"I should go." He stood, shoving the bench back, his porridge still untouched.

"I'll be here when you get back. Just come find me, okay?"

He nodded. It was a nice offer, but not one he intended to take. Without Mal he had nothing.

———

No one looked his way when he stopped by the kitchen, loading up a sack with enough food for a day or two. If he had to do this, he wasn't going to "get it over with" like so many others had before him. He'd give Mal the full day. Take him to his favorite spot, let him bask in the sunshine one last time.

A full day. After twenty-five years Mal had earned at least that much.

He found Mal sprawled across the sand in his enclosure, his wings spread out to capture as much sun as he could, a small iron chain around his ankle all that kept him from flying away.

Gray remembered the first time they'd placed a chain around Mal's ankle. He was just a few weeks old and starting to stretch his wings. But he couldn't be allowed to escape. Dragons were too precious. And too dangerous.

So they'd placed that chain around his ankle and when he made his first tentative attempts to fly it pulled him back to the ground, kept him from flying away until he was big enough to take Gray with him. Only then was he allowed to fly free.

Now that he was large enough no chain could keep him on the ground, he never even tried to fly on his own. Gray wished he would. It would be better. Easier.

"Hey there, buddy. You up for a flight?" He stepped close enough to grab the stick he kept in Mal's enclosure and used it to scratch the skin above his eyes. Mal leaned into it with a soft sigh before finally pulling his wings in and lumbering to a standing position.

Gray wasn't the only one with scars. When Mal stood the sun caught the thick ridge of tissue that ran across his chest from where another dragon had raked his hide with its talons. Gray had thought they were done that day, but somehow Mal had not only managed to defeat the other dragon but land safely in a field, careful even in his agony to protect Gray.

It had taken three months for the wound to fully heal.

And then it was back to the battle. The next wound was just a nick to the wing membrane. Two weeks out for that one. The scar above his eye, a day. The slice to his tail, two days.

Gray could've spent the rest of the day cataloging Mal's scars, but Mal nudged him with his snout, pushing him towards the riding gear stacked neatly in the corner. Gray had spent hours working the leather until it was as soft as he could make it. And he'd badgered the harness maker until the leather fit Mal perfectly. He ran his hands along its length, smelling the worked leather, remembering.

Twenty-five years. How do you say goodbye after that long?

He forced himself to smile and joke as he placed the riding harness on Mal. No one was lingering near the enclosure, but he knew they were watching, making sure he was going to "do the right thing".

As he finished, the commander arrived. "You'll need to tell us where you left him when you return. So we can send a team to…you know."

Anger flared again, but Gray tamped it down and just nodded.

"You wouldn't be the first rider who wanted to let him go instead, you know."

Gray didn't look his way.

"But you can't do that. He'd terrorize the countryside. We'd have to go after him."

Gray wanted to argue. He wanted to say that Mal could be fine for months before the next Forgetting. To say that he deserved better than this.

But just like he wasn't the first rider who'd wanted to let his dragon fly free, he wasn't the first to make those arguments. This was the safest decision. The best decision.

For everyone except Mal.

The commander patted his back awkwardly. "Try to leave him somewhere it's easy for the team to reach if you can."

Gray's hand clenched into a fist, but he didn't move or respond as the commander turned and left.

Mal scratched at the sand, the only sign of his impatience. He dipped his head and nudged Gray as if saying, "Hurry up. Let's go play."

For the briefest of moments Gray considered letting someone else do it. He could understand the temptation. Let some other rider fly Mal away and return alone. Let some other rider be the one to repay twenty-five years of dedication with betrayal.

But asking someone else to ride Mal would distress him, and that was absolutely not what Gray wanted, so he scrambled into the saddle and paused for a long moment to look across the vast sprawl of the compound.

He didn't want his youth back—he'd probably waste it worse than he had the first time around. And he didn't want one last battle full of blood and fire and death—he knew now that glory was a myth and that killing a man in battle was no better than killing a man in the street.

He had no big ambitions, no dreams, no goals.

He just wanted time. Time to sit with Mal and enjoy the

sun on his skin. Time to soar through the clouds. Time to enjoy the life they'd earned with blood and death.

Mal turned his head until one golden eye was fixed on Gray's face and then he looked up at the sky and back again once more, all that lively intelligence of his on full display.

Gray swallowed. It made it that much harder that today Mal knew who Gray was and would wait for the command to fly.

"Go." Gray nudged Mal with his knees and Mal beat his powerful wings, faltering slightly as he rose from the ground, his right wing beating a little less powerfully than the left, struggling with the extra weight he'd slowly acquired over the last few years away from the battle field.

But then they were climbing, reaching towards the clouds, and the world fell away. It was just Gray and Mal soaring high above everyone and everything.

There was a place Mal had always loved. A large lake ringed by mountains, not too far from the compound. It was beautiful. And it was quiet. Mal could plunge into the lake and then dry off on the lake's edge in the soft green grass. Gray tried to take him there as often as he could, but it was far enough away that that wasn't very often.

Mal was as eager as a young fledgling when he realized where they were going. He flew faster than he had in weeks. Gray finally let his tears fall as they flew too high for anyone to see them.

When they reached the lake Mal tucked his wings in tight, and dropped towards the water, Gray cussing and laughing as they plummeted into the center, water crashing away from them in all directions.

Gray slid off Mal's back and made for the safety of shore as Mal rolled and splashed around, frisky as a puppy.

He sat on the shore and watched, smiling at his friend's enjoyment. He would have stayed in the water, but as much as Mal had learned to be careful with talons and tail, he still didn't appreciate how easily a human could drown.

When Mal was finally done in the water he waddled onto the shore and spread out by Gray's side, wings stretched wide to capture the sun. Gray wiped him down, carefully removing the excess water and weeds that had tangled themselves in his talons and tail.

They laid down side-by-side, eyes closed to let the midday sun dry them the rest of the way.

As the sun soaked into his skin and Mal's rumbling snores filled the air, Gray thought back to all the moments they'd had together. That first time he'd seen Mal and realized that this was his dragon. No one else's. *His.* Those large golden eyes so big compared to those scrawny little legs.

And those times early on when he'd been so frustrated trying to train Mal that he'd wanted to scream. He'd been burned and cut and deprived of sleep for weeks on end, wondering what he was thinking wanting to be a dragonrider. Wondering if it was too late to join the cavalry.

But then one day Mal put his head in Gray's lap and looked up at him with eyes full of trust and love for the first time and he never doubted again.

And that first flight…

Oh, the sheer thrill of it, the freedom. Soaring through the air…

And then came all the nights when he'd been hurt or Mal had been hurt and they'd insisted on being there for each other. He smiled remembering the time Mal had almost given a nurse a heart attack when he stuck his head through the tent flap trying to find Gray. Almost took the whole tent down.

And the battles. The battles were there, too, of course. The way they worked together as a team, moving and thinking as one. Surviving because they had absolute trust in one another. Because they were friends.

How many lazy afternoons had they spent like this one, lying in the sun and letting it soak all their cares away?

Not enough. Not enough by far.

And now…

Now it was time. To say goodbye. To end things before it was too late. Before all those good memories were replaced with bad.

He stood, careful not to disturb Mal, and reached for his bag, for the sharp knife tucked away inside.

Gray sat at the edge of the lake and watched the sun set over the mountains, painting the sky in brilliant shades of pink and purple, the knife still clutched in his hand.

How many sunsets had he missed in his life? Too busy to stop and appreciate the simple beauty the world had to offer. Too focused on the next moment to appreciate the current one.

He'd had twenty-five years with one of the most amazing creatures in the world. With a companion who would give anything in exchange for simple love and loyalty. A companion who'd sacrifice his very life if asked.

How many years had he asked that of Mal and taken for granted that Mal would be there for him no matter what?

Too many.

Gray watched the sun sink further, but still he didn't move.

Mal's scales caught the last of the setting sun, reflecting its light in a thousand different directions, and Gray bowed his head.

Some moments once passed can never be reclaimed. Some choices once made can never be taken back. This was one of those choices.

But he knew it was the right one, no matter the consequences. He sheathed the knife and stood, wiping the dirt from his pants with shaking hands.

"Come on, Mal. It's time for us to go."

Mal opened one eye, making his lack of enthusiasm plain.

Gray pushed at his shoulder. "Come on. We have to get moving before they come looking for us."

Mal closed his eye again. He'd never been one who enjoyed flying at night, even if the moon was full, but Gray nudged and prodded until he finally gave in and stood, wings shaking as he stretched and yawned, those large teeth on full display.

It took a few minutes to get the harness back on him since it had stiffened up after its time in the lake, but they managed eventually.

Grey knew they'd never let him come back as a commander or a trainer or anything else after this. And that they'd probably send riders after him, too. But he didn't care.

As Mal launched into the sky, Gray smiled.

It could be months or even years until Mal's next attack and Mal deserved those years. He'd earned them. He'd given his life to Gray and now Gray was going to give it back.

Because that's what friends do for one another. They stay together, no matter what.

Mal had lived in his world, now it was time for him to live in Mal's. He turned Mal towards the distant mountains where wild dragons soared and men feared to tread, ready for the next adventure with his best friend.

OUR STORY

This is our story, they tell me.

Long ago we lived in another place. A place of peace and beauty. But then the fires came. And the floods. And we had to leave that place. We traveled for a hundred days and a hundred nights across the water. And then for another hundred days and another hundred nights we walked across the land we had found until we reached the hillside with the snake and the tree.

We knew then that we were home because the Gods had foretold this place. They had come to us in visions, they had guarded us on our journey to our new home. They gave us the tree to build our temple on the hill so that we might worship them for all our days.

We sit now in that very temple and we give our thanks for the home the Gods provided.

"Are there no other stories?" I ask.

No. None. This is the only story. Our story.

But after I leave them, after I walk away from the white-washed halls of the building that sits atop the hillside, I wander down to the river. There I find the old crone who fishes every day, her hands and toes webbed to better catch her prey. She has no name. None that she shares.

But we spend hours together in the summer sun, side-by-side, fishing, me with my pole and line, her with her clever hands.

I tell her our story. I tell her this is the only one.

She laughs.

Yours is not the only story. Long ago my people lived in another place, too. Deep under the water where it was salty and dark. But over time there were those born who needed the light and the air. Who needed the water to run fresh and clear and free of the tang of salt.

Those children of the light moved away from their home in the deep water, and they found the land. They found the streams and the lakes. They traveled along those streams until they found a place with a tree on top of a hill.

A tree that gave shelter and food. A friend. They knew then this was their new home. And they settled here in the shade of the tree, fishing and hunting, one with the land.

Until the day the others arrived. And they too saw the tree. But rather than shelter in the shade of the tree they cut the tree down and built their temple where it had stood. In honor of their Gods they drove away those who had come before.

I leave her and go back to the temple. I tell them of her story, but they shake their heads.

No. That is not our story. That is another story. A story of the other. We have told you our story. Our story of might and destiny. There is no other story.

Once more, I leave the temple, but this time my feet take me to the market, loud and wild with all the voices and all the animals and goods for sale. I find my favorite stall, the one that belongs to the woman who wears layer after layer of cloth wound around and flowing from her body. The woman who paints the lids of her eyes and her lips in colors I've never seen before.

I sit with her as she chats and barters and weaves rugs of such beautiful colors it makes my eyes hurt.

I tell her our story. I tell her it is the only story.

She laughs and her laugh is like the wind chimes that hang outside my room, clear and pure.

That may be your story, she says. But it is not my story. My people lived in a land of plenty for thousands upon thousands of years. We learned and we studied and we acquired all of the knowledge of the world. Until the day the raiders came and they burned it all to the ground and we fled.

For many years we traveled. Here. There. Stopping for a year or two or ten. But always we pushed onward to somewhere new, somewhere different. We split apart and lost one another along the way until the whole world was ours and yet nowhere was ours.

Until I alone traveled to this city with its temple upon a hill. And I found a place amongst those in the market. A place where I could weave my rugs and listen to the silly tales of foolish children who think their story is the only one.

She smiles to take away the sting of her words, but I leave anyway, driven back to the temple.

I tell them her story, but they laugh at me.

We are not wanderers. We are a people with a direction. Driven by the Gods. We were never lost. We just weren't home yet. We have told you our story. There is no other story.

I leave the temple once more and I walk to the edge of town where there are taverns and inns. I sit on a stool in the back of the bar where my uncle works and I tell him our story. But a man at the bar tells me I'm wrong as he drinks his ale.

That may be your story, little one, but it is not mine. Mine is a tale of adventure. I don't know who birthed me. I don't who raised me. I was on my own from as long as I could remember. I had friends, but they came and went. I somehow found food and shelter and grew until I was a young man, old enough to be hired to work as a caravan guard. I have traveled ever since. From town to town, country to country. I have heard many stories told in many different voices and tongues.

Your story may be yours, but it is not mine. And it is not hers. Or his. Or theirs. Your story is just one of the drops in the ocean. One of the stars in the sky. Your story is a story, but it is not the story.

Late that night I finally return home. My mother's mother sits by the fire, her hands wrapped in cloths like they've always been, her eyes rheumy with age. I tell her about the story I learned at temple. And I tell her about the others I spoke to that day, each with their own story. I ask her what my story is. Is it the story they tell at the temple? Or do I have a different story.

She pulls me into her lap and I cuddle against her side as she starts to speak.

They will tell you there is only one story. They will tell you there is only one truth. But they are wrong.

She unwinds the cloth from around her hands and I see the faintest hint of a web between each finger as she speaks.

My father's father's people traveled for a hundred days and a hundred nights and then a hundred more to reach this place. My mother's mother's people came from the water back when salt tasted sweet. My mother's father found his way here from a place far, far away where all the knowledge of the world once lived before it was burned to nothing by ignorant fools who didn't know what it was they destroyed. And my father's mother never knew her people. She was taken in by a kind couple who found her alone in the night babbling in a tongue none had ever heard.

They are all a part of our story.

They are all a part of you.

But your story, my child, is your own. Your story is the one you choose to tell. It's the threads in the tapestry that you choose to see whether that be a single strand or many.

As I fall asleep that night, I think about what my grandmother said. About how all of the stories are mine. About how I can choose whichever one I want.

And I smile.

Because they are all my story. And yet, none of them are *my* story.

My story is yet to be written.

ABOUT THE AUTHOR

You can reach M.H. Lee at <u>mhleewriter@gmail.com</u>

www.ingramcontent.com/pod-product-compliance
Lightning Source LLC
Chambersburg PA
CBHW070950190726
48292CB00004B/1413